VALERIE HOLMES

THE VALIANT FOOL

Complete and Unabridged

LINFORD
Leicester

First published in Great Britain in 2009

First Linford Edition
published 2009

British Library CIP Data

Holmes, Valerie.
   The valiant fool
   1. Love stories.
   2. Large type books.
   I. Title
   823.9'2–dc22

ISBN 978–1–84782–643–5

Published by
F. A. Thorpe (Publishing)
Anstey, Leicestershire

Set by Words & Graphics Ltd.
Anstey, Leicestershire
Printed and bound in Great Britain by
T. J. International Ltd., Padstow, Cornwall

This book is printed on acid-free paper

THE VALIANT FOOL

Emma Frinton, a captain's daughter, is forced to live in reduced circumstances in a humble cottage in the small fishing village of Ebton, when the French imprison her father. Emma and her mother, Lydia, accept leaving their beloved home in Whitby, but neither of them anticipates the consequences of Emma's kindly actions when she stumbles across an injured man on the dunes. In saving Montgomery Wild's life, she unwittingly finds the key to unlock their family's future.

1

Emma hurried along the edge of the dunes. Darkness crept over the beach as tiny ice crystals started to form upon the sand. It was a harsh frost tonight and deadly to anyone caught out in it, but Emma had no intention of that happening.

Knowing that her mother would be worried about her safety made her hurry even more. Guilt played at her conscience because she should have been coming down the road and not wandering on her own over the dunes. Emma was returning from a mercy mission. She had walked along the beach to the lighthouse to see the coastguard's family who lived in the house two hundred paces before the Gannet Rock Light. It had been a tiring day, which she had not regretted — only the sadness that hung over her that she hadn't better news to return with.

Her foot slipped on the softer sand and she stumbled as she made her way across to the path which would take her up into the fishing village that she now called home . . . at least it was for her immediate future. Her vision dimmed as the light faded. One minute she was struggling up to the path and the next she fell full length against the cold fine grained sand, her foot caught on what she presumed to be the root of the wild grass that grew around this hostile terrain.

'Stupid fool,' Emma muttered as she stood up brushing the sand from her skirt. 'Ouch.' She caught her cold finger on the edge of the sharp grass, and glanced down at the offending blade when it became visible. She stared at the spot where she had tripped and realised her toe had not caught on a root but something much larger. Emma leaned forward, and gasped. A leg laid askew the track. She bent low; the outline of a body became visible.

Hesitantly she prodded the man's torso which was half hidden by the long grass between two of the sandy mounds. There was no response. She stood straight. 'A body!' Emma tried to stifle the feeling of panic which was growing within her. 'I might have found a body — a dead body!' She turned, ready to run, but then heard a groan emanate from area of the ground behind her. Emma glanced back, eyes wide, as the figure of a man stood to his full height, silhouetted against the vast expanse of the distant sea. He quickly stooped again, holding out a shaky hand towards her.

Instinctively she took hold of the hand. 'Who are you, sir?' Her voice was as unsteady as his grip, but he tried to hold on tightly. He was either frightened or injured; Emma knew that he desperately needed her help.

'Hide me . . . please . . . they'll come.' He stepped toward her, using her hand to steady him. He was so cold, wet and alone. She felt her heart leap a beat. She wanted to help him, but the villagers hated strangers; she knew this from her own experience. They hated and distrusted the coastguard. The family were, like them, not local to the area. The poor man lay ill abed after an attack when trying to apprehend a man carrying contraband. He was lucky to live but his family would have suffered if not for the charity of Emma and her mother. She stared at the fallen figure, his breath heavy and uneven.

'I will try to help you, sir, but you must come with me. I will take you to a place of shelter, behind our cottage and hide you, but you will have to be honest with me and tell me what is amiss. Who are you running from, the pressgang?' She walked him slowly along the path.

'The tracks, they'll see the tracks!' The fear in his voice was palpable.

'No need to fret about that, they'll be lost to the sea and the night. Who seeks you, sir?' she repeated.

'The militia, they'll hang me without trial. Help me and I shall reward you. I can do that generously once this nightmare is over. I shall be very generous upon my word.' He was shaking and Emma realised that he was not fretful, but desperately cold. He needed help, and quickly. She would find out the right and wrong of it once she had done what she could to save him from his immediate predicament.

* * *

By the time they had traversed the ground and skirted the village, he was cold as a living being could be whilst still clinging to life. Emma made a rash decision and decided he needed the warmth of a fire if he were to recover. Entering the cottage slowly, Emma helped the stranger over the threshold and towards the low fire her mother had left burning in the hearth. The man was pale and shivering. He could not have survived a night in the outhouse so, despite her better judgement, Emma had decided to bring him into their home and hope her mother would understand why. Emma helped him remove his greatcoat. It was heavy with the damp from the previous days of rain. This man had not been able to get dry for some time. Underneath this Emma was surprised to see he wore a uniform, not of the militia but a deep green coloured jacket. The militia, it appeared, were hunting a soldier — but why? Unless, of course, he was a deserter. She gritted her teeth. Was she harbouring a traitor and a coward? He shivered uncontrollably. Pushing all thought of this from her mind she pulled off the jacket leaving him quivering in a grubby, once white, shirt.

'Hide them, please. I need to lose the uniform.' He looked up at her with tired blue eyes. 'Don't destroy it, please, but hide it for me, in that I am a marked man, so place it safe where it will not be found . . . '

'What is going on here, Emma Frinton?' Emma dropped the jacket, startled by the appearance of her mother in the doorway of the cottage. The cold blast of salty sea air followed her mother inside.

'Shut the door quickly . . . please,' the shaky voice almost whispered.

Lydia closed it behind her, slamming a bolt across it; in her hand she held a poker and gestured for Emma to come over to her. 'Here quickly, Emma!' She waved her hand frantically. 'I've been looking for you for half an hour. I didn't see you coming along the road.'

'No, I cut across the dunes,' Emma stared at her mother who let out a low sigh. She was always warning her about walking on the dunes on her own. She didn't trust the locals any more than they did her. On top of that there was the danger of unknown tides and the soft sand. Some said when wet it hid spots where a man could be sucked down, anchored by his legs, helpless to stop an approaching sea from drowning him.

'Haven't my words warned you

enough? Now, look where it has led. We have a fugitive under our own roof. Girl you are so like . . . '

'Father, I know. You told me.' Emma smiled, but her mother shook her head.

'Aye, and look where that's got him . . . a prisoner of war.' She sniffed and stared at the stranger.

'Ma, he's sick, he needs help. We can't turn him out on a night like this . . . it would be cold blooded murder.' Emma looked at her mother, knowing they were somehow being drawn into this man's problems, as if they had not enough of their own.

'The empha . . . sis, being on . . . c . . . c . . . cold.' He was leaning toward the fire, hugging his arms to his body.

Lydia came forward and placed the end of the poker under his chin lifting his head up. The light of the fire illuminated his face. Emma could see clearly the deep rings under his eyes, a drawn expression and grazed skin. 'You've been on the run for quite a while, young man. Why?' Her mother's voice was firm; she did not remove the poker.

He glanced at her. 'I could not wrestle a mouse in my current state so there is no need for that. I am not a fugitive. I am not a coward, miss,' he said directly to Emma. 'I am a man who needs help. I cannot be of use to you unless I am fit and well again. Please hide me here until I can warm my bones through again, or you may have to explain how you came to be harbouring a corpse.' His dull eyes glanced up at Lydia.

'Is it not bad enough that we are harbouring a man that the militia has been scouting the roads looking for? Silas told me they are combing the land between Stangcliffe and Gorebeck. They think he has tried to make for the coast to find a boat to Baytown or Whitby. They went through every cottage in Ebton not two hours ago. Every boat was accounted for. So what is it you have done, man, and do not lie to me or I will split your skull with my very own poker!' Lydia pushed it a little so it nudged his chin.

He closed his eyes. Lydia glanced to Emma as they did not understand what he was doing. Emma had not heard her mother, a gentlewoman, speak so before. They were distracted only momentarily; neither saw his arm reach up so swiftly. The poker was wrenched from her mother's hand. She took a step back and shielded her daughter. The door behind them was bolted and their escape blocked as the man stood, with poker in hand, glaring at the two of them. Lydia swore under her breath. Somehow, from somewhere deep inside he had found an inner strength, and she had grievously misjudged him.

2

Captain Gregory Wild watched the sergeant walk hesitantly into his office. 'Well then, Blunt. Tell me you have found him, man!' his voice boomed out. He saw the sergeant wince, but felt no sympathy for him. He had been paid, and paid well to do a job, and he had obviously failed abysmally.

'We looked from town to coast. Went through all the cottages in the hamlets and still no trace of him. He must have taken to the open moor, marshes or dunes. He couldn't be hiding anywhere with folks around here. They don't care for strangers; more likely to attack them or turn them out. We'd have found him for sure.' The sergeant shrugged his arched shoulders. 'It isn't like he knows these parts; he'd stand out like a sore thumb.'

'Stand tall, man. Don't come in here

like some defeated hound whimpering at my ankles. You have had eight of our finest scouring the area and you cannot find the trace of a half starved toff in a rough terrain? I should have sent the groom out instead; at least he trained as a gamekeeper. Perhaps he could have tracked him down. It's going to freeze out there tonight. Tomorrow you go and bring back his frozen corpse and no more excuses. I want him buried in an unmarked grave where he cannot shame our family name.' He looked back down at his desk, aware that his sergeant had not moved.

'Sir, he could have got away in a boat with an accomplice. Perhaps he did not run alone.'

'Ask the coastguard, Packman, if he's heard anything or seen anyone on his patrol.' Gregory looked up, a stillness filled the room before he erupted, slamming his pipe down onto the desk and shouting at the man in front of him. 'You had better pray he has not escaped or I'll have your stripes! Go, get your rest and start the search as soon as day dawns! This time do not fail me.'

'Yes, sir!' The sergeant backed away. 'Packman is still not fully recovered, sir,' he added. 'He is still unable to walk more than a few feet and riding is out of the question.'

'This land is goin' to ruin whilst men take to their beds like a bunch of mild mannered maidens. Hell's teeth!'

The sergeant left the room. Gregory heard him bark his own orders at the men. He smiled with one corner of his mouth. 'Good, he'll find him; Monty's days were numbered . . . at last.'

* * *

Emma grabbed her mother's hand, as much to pull her behind her if the man attacked them. Instead, he dropped the poker onto the hearth and sat back down. 'Ladies, I have no desire to hurt you. Neither do I wish to be hurt further. If you would kindly allow me some food and rest I shall go on my way before dawn and you can forget that I ever existed.' He rested his head in his hands as he stared at the small flickering flames.

Lydia walked over to the kettle that rested on a hotplate at the side of the fire. 'Emma, set the table for tea. This man needs a warm drink. Sir, you shall come into our bedchamber and strip out of those wet things. You can wear my husband's old trousers and shirt for tonight. We shall make you at least half human again.'

Emma watched her mother lead him into their own bedchamber; it was the only other room in the cottage and was thought by the people of the hamlet to be a luxury, as most families existed within the single roomed cottages. They had a room to live in, one to sleep in and even an outhouse to take in washing. This, to them, was poverty, yet people envied them the luxury they had. Perspective in life skewed all and everything, Emma reflected.

Lydia came back through. 'He will be ready in a few minutes. What news of Allan Packman? Has he recovered?'

Emma shook her head. He seems to want to sleep most of the time. Mary is worried sick and has the baby to look after. The townsfolk won't offer to help them because they see him as an enemy of the free trade, yet they can't see it is they who are being traitors by giving the French our coin.' Emma shook her head. If only Father had stayed they would still be in their old home on the outskirts of Whitby. Now they had to exist in this small cottage and rent out their fine house in order to keep a living.

'You can't blame people for being short-sighted when they have families to feed.' Lydia would not be drawn into politics, which made Emma miss her father even more, because whenever he came to shore he would tell her all about what was wrong in the world, and discuss the affairs of government with her as if she were a man. Lydia did not approve of him filling her daughter's head with such notions, but only expressed her disapproval by abstinence from their debates.

'Do you trust him . . . the stranger?' Emma whispered.

'Trust? What has that to do with anything? It appears we have been placed in his path. I cannot turn him out and it is our Christian duty to help him, so help him we shall, but I want to know what it is we are protecting. If he is a traitor or a coward, I shall hand him in myself.' Lydia poured the boiling water into a porcelain pot. Emma placed the china cups and saucers next to it.

The door opened and both women stared at him as, by the poor light of the oil lamps, it looked as though their husband and father were back with them, but it was a fleeting hope, or wish, because as he stepped forward, it was obvious from the shortness of the shirt's sleeve and the gathering of fabric about his trousers' waist band, which was clearly measured for a more ample figure.

'Sit down and drink before you fall down.' Lydia pulled out a chair.

'What is your name, sir?' Emma asked as they seated themselves at the table.

Lydia cut a piece of fresh bread and lay it before him with a cut of mutton.

'Montgomery Wild, Miss Frinton,' he replied, before sinking his teeth into the cold mutton.' He looked at her and repeated, 'Frinton!'

'How do you know her name?' Lydia asked.

Emma smiled at her mother's shocked expression; clearly she had forgotten shouting it as she entered the cottage.

'You introduced us in a manner of speaking, ma'am.' He drank from the cup, placing it as carefully as he could back on its saucer, his hand still shaking. 'You have fine tastes, not at all what I would expect from . . . ' He glanced around the sparse room.

'Perhaps, like your good self we are

not at all what we appear to be on first inspection.' He nodded at Lydia's words and Emma could see that their new friend would be that, for they all appeared to be in the wrong place. 'You will need to be warm tonight, Mr Montgomery Wild. We will wrap you well by the fire and you shall have your rest. How long has it been since you were dry and warm?'

'Are you a traitor?' Emma asked outright. Lydia shot her a sharp look but Montgomery looked at her, meeting her eyes with his.

'No, miss, I am not. I am a man who has been wronged and I intend to right a ruined reputation. I am . . . was a Captain in rank, not at sea, like I believe your husband is, but in the special forces of the army, ma'am.'

Lydia glared at him. 'How do you presume to make such an assumption about my husband?'

'Fate is a queer mistress, sometimes she tosses people aside, then at others she puts them in place . . . or perhaps

God does.' He sipped his drink.

'I think your brain has been addled, sir. How do you know of my husband?' Lydia was becoming clearly agitated.

Montgomery continued, 'However, justice may not be as straight forward as I had supposed it to be. It would appear that a man I trusted has played me foul, so I am at this time a man without friends in this region.' He looked across at Lydia. 'I will repay your kindness, but it is not being bereft of friendship here that is the danger, but rather the presence of an enemy.'

'Then perhaps we shall be your friends and help you in your mission to clear your name, Captain.' Emma's voice caused both Montgomery and Lydia to stare at her. Lydia's eyes shot upwards in a silent rebuke, but through tired eyes Montgomery smiled at her.

'Emma, The Valliant,' he said softly.

'The Valliant Fool,' her mother snapped out, then flushed at her outburst for she was clearly disturbed by his presence and frightened for her daughter's safety.

Montgomery chuckled at the comment. 'Not a fool, miss. I have good news . . . ' but he coughed at the effort of talking and the shivering began again with a vengeance. Both women stood up and supported him.

'Roll out the spare mattress, Emma. This man needs warmth and sleep.' Lydia turned to him. 'Captain, your good news will have to wait till morning. Then I will want all my questions answering.'

He closed his eyes and nodded, obviously not wishing to speak anymore. The next minutes were filled with activity, arranging a makeshift bed. They helped him almost fall onto it. Lydia tucked him up as Emma washed their cups up and placed them carefully back in the cupboard. Lydia then went to the bedchamber. 'Come, Emma, leave him to rest,' she ordered after her.

Emma walked by the sleepy figure. He tugged her skirt and she crouched low next to him. 'What is it, Mr

Montgomery Wild?'

'There is nothing foolish . . . in being valiant . . . for a good cause.' He tried to find the energy to grin, but everything seemed such an effort to him that he looked as though he had little left at all.

'Are you one, a good man, Montgomery, or do you play us both as fools, sir?' he tucked his arm back into the bedding.

'Yes, I am. My friends call me Monty. I do not lie to you, I swear.' His voice was very faint.

'You don't have any friends, Monty.' She stroked his cheek; it felt warmer than it had.

'I do now.' He leaned his cheek into her hand and he closed his eyes as if at peace.

'Emma!' Her mother's voice shook her but it did not cause him to flinch in the slightest. He had drifted off into oblivion.

'Coming, Mother.' Emma walked to the adjoining doorway glancing back down at the stranger who slept soundly, and had not moved his head more than half an inch from where she had rested it in her hand. Just as their life had taken a sudden turn once she they had heard of her father's fate, it appeared now was yet another unexpected twist of fate. Wherever it would lead she did not know.

3

The violent knocking on the door woke Monty from a deep and peaceful sleep. The shutters were still closed and the fire had died away. 'Open up, Damn you! Or we shall break this door down!' a man's voice shouted.

Monty stood up quickly, too quickly for his head to gain its senses; he swayed and placed his hand against the wall to steady himself. Lydia appeared from her bedchamber in a lace bonnet, wrapping a shawl around her thin body which was covered by a thick white cotton nightdress. Her stance held a natural grace, one that was more usually found in a lady of good breeding and position. She had been trained how to hold herself correctly. She did not stoop like many a woman did after years of doing chores or hard work.

'I'll give myself up,' he offered, but there was no conviction within his voice, and a petrified look of desperation in his eyes. 'I have caused you enough distress already.'

'Mother, he can't,' Emma whispered, as she looked at the pathetically defeated expression on Montgomery's face. Standing in her nightdress in the open doorway, she stared at him, and he her, realising her own appearance at that point was equally as vulnerable.

'Lord, help us.' Lydia glanced back at her daughter as the pounding on the door resumed. 'You, sir, climb into my bed. Your uniform is hidden under the mattress. Emma, you sit yourself on the side of the bed as if you have just woken up, and wrap yourself in your shawl and cover yourself, girl. In the name of decency, whatever next!' She turned to the door staring at her daughter who wore only her nightdress, no cap and bare feet.

Emma blushed as she saw Monty was looking at her also.

Her mother yelled loudly, 'Give a woman a chance, man. It's the middle of the night!' she was almost screaming as the door gave way a little under the heavy bombardment the soldier was inflicting upon it.

Montgomery did not waste any time. Emma watched her mother turn back the bedding on the floor as if she had just woken from it. 'What do we tell them?'

'Shut the door, girl, and hopefully they'll not disturb my daughter and her . . . husband in their bedchamber.' She waved her arm frantically at Emma to retreat into her room, whilst opening the shutters and letting the first shards of daylight into the small building. Reluctantly, she removed the bolt from the door and allowed two of the militia's soldiers to enter.

'What took yer so long to open up, and explain, woman, why the door should be barred.' The soldier stepped over to the fire and, with his foot, nudged the mattress on the floor. The first soldier looked around the cottage helping himself to a chunk of their bread which he broke off the cob with his dirty hands.

Lydia looked at him and wanted to call him an uncouth and common man but knew it would be stupid to provoke him. 'Because it's night time and I don't want just anybody to open the door, burst in and scare me to death in my bed.' She glanced down at the floor where the bedding was laid out. 'If yer don't mind I'd prefer not to have sand kicked in my bedding.'

'Well day has dawned. What's through there?' he pointed to the door and asked, as he opened and looked inside a cupboard and nodded to the other room.

'The bedchamber,' she said, absently as she rolled up her mattress and placed it carefully back into the other cupboard.

'Then why were you sleeping on the floor?' he asked, and put a hand on the door's latch.

'Because my daughter and her

husband have the bed in there. They are not long wed, and need privacy.' She blushed as the two men laughed. Whatever was she saying? Lydia was filled with both bewilderment and disgust at these poor excuses for soldiers. Her husband said it was an honour to wear a uniform; it made a man respect what he was about, and that he fought for his country. She continued, 'And besides, I like to be by the warmth of the fire.' She prodded the embers with the poker and was rewarded with a glow, then a flame.

'Well, you should get yourself a man. You're not beyond it yet!'

Lydia gasped, and fought to control the words that filled her brain from pouring out of her mouth.

The soldier flung the door open wide. Holding a pistol in his hand he entered the room. The two figures were entwined in an embrace within the covers. As the soldier and Lydia entered they quickly separated, and Emma screamed loudly.

'Hush, woman! What be the meanin' of this,' Monty drawled. He sounded drunk, his voice slurred. 'Can't a man lie in 'is own bed with 'is own woman without bein' disturbed?' He rose up on one elbow, rubbing his face with his hand, but Emma sat forward blocking the soldier's clear view of him.

'Lucky sod,' the soldier said, as he stared at Emma. Her dark hair hung loose over her shoulders as she held the quilted cover up to her neck, which also served to help to obscure the view of Monty. The soldier winked at his friend who was behind Lydia.

'Nice, eh?' They laughed and turned, muttering something to each other which resulted in a raucous guffaw from one of them and agreement in the other. 'You should be out earning a crust for your family with the other fishermen,' the older man said, as he glanced around the sparse room. The other looked under the bed and in a chest, shrugged his shoulders and left the room.

'He's not well this morning,' Emma said defiantly.

'Aye, and the band sang 'believe that it if yer like'.' The soldier walked out.

Lydia paused to glare at them both and wagged a finger at Emma, but she had to leave them in the room, without saying a word, closing the door behind her to see the strangers out.

Emma flushed deeply as she sat in her bed, and looked down at Monty lying next to her. He looked more rested than the previous night and had stopped shaking. Fortunately the fever that she and Lydia thought would follow had not arrived; he had a strong constitution, her mother had told her. A dark fringe had fallen over one of his eyes, so instinctively she flicked it out of his face.

'Thank you,' he remarked quietly.

'You look better. You obviously needed warmth and sleep, but you have a lot to explain to us. We have placed ourselves in a perilous situation on your behalf, yet we don't yet know why.'

'I will explain in full as soon as they have left the village.' He looked up at her and a sparkle of life had reappeared in his eyes which had been missing the previous evening. 'I could have died out there. You saved my life, Emma, last night and again now.' He flicked the end of her hair as it lay against her back. 'You are beautiful, Miss Emma Frinton, in mind and body.' He smiled at her.

Emma flushed deeply, and suddenly became aware of the situation fate had placed them in. She reached for her shawl and pulled it around her as she swung her feet over the side of the bed and into her slippers, instantly standing up and stepping back from the bed.

'I'm sorry, that was presumptuous of me.' He sat up, resting his elbows on his raised knees. 'I was not trying to make an inappropriate approach, just stating what I see to be the obvious truth.'

'No, I understand you must think me a . . . hoyden.' Emma didn't really know what he would think of her, jumping into bed and hugging him like that. She had wanted to protect him, hide him, without thinking rationally — decently, just following her own instinct and spontaneity, but everything had happened so fast that they had been swept along into a situation, and she wondered if the cost of that would be that they would have to live a lie. The consequences of their well meaning subterfuge had just begun to sink in. Whatever would her mother make of it? On top of all their other problems they were now entwined in this stranger's too. She tried to block the memory of his embrace as he had held her so firmly, her own base nature had responded with a thrill of excitement. She was behaving badly.

Emma faced him. She looked at his outstretched arm, she was gong to be defiant and firm with him, insisting he leave them as soon as the soldiers left Ebton, but then her eyes caught sight of a red raw ring around his wrist. Her demeanour softened and she had to know. 'Who did that to you?'

'Miss Frinton, I could not begin to think anything ill of you or your character. You have acted with the utmost kindness, nothing else. I do not believe you could ever willingly be or understand the nature of a hoyden, not by choice.'

She looked away, and gripped the shawl to her, feeling ill at ease but was grateful when he continued speaking on a different subject. Her mother would no doubt have plenty to say on the subject once the soldiers were beyond earshot.

'The marks on my wrists are a gift from the local justice of the militia. I am to be hounded as a fugitive by my own cousin, Captain Gregory Wild. I have been named and shamed, for his financial gain, and I shall not accept it. Somehow I will clear my name, but first I need to be free to do so.' He stood up and straightened the sheets.

The door was flung open revealing the irate figure of Lydia. 'You, sir, have the nerve and the luck of the devil himself. You have inconvenienced us greatly and now my daughter's reputation has been ruined. What possessed you, Emma, to climb into bed with . . . with a . . . Was it not bad enough you should be half naked in a bedchamber with him?'

'I am not half naked, Mother. That is exaggeration!' Emma was so embarrassed. Her mother was about to remark further when Montgomery spoke up.

'I am a gentleman, Mrs Frinton, an innocent man who has done work for His Majesty's Government. Who has served him loyally and has been falsely accused of cowardice and running from the field of battle, when in fact I was taken by a small group of my own men; the very group of men who bore witness to my running. I was left behind enemy lines, was captured, imprisoned and was then paroled, exchanged for a captured French officer. All for what? I knew not. I was disgraced in front of my men and sent home to face the consequences, but I jumped ship. I headed here and sought the assistance of my cousin Gregory, only to have the hounds set on me by him. He conveniently believes that I am guilty!'

Montgomery raised an eyebrow as Lydia took in his words. 'Now the good news I was unable to impart yesterday is for your ears, Ma'am.'

'Speak it, man,' Lydia said, still short of temper and, Emma thought, frightened by the latest turn of events.

'I am also a man who has come here with another mission which is why I made for this small village. Whilst in that prison I made a friend. Who would have thought that miles away from my own home I would meet a man who hailed from not ten miles from my childhood residence, that of our estate south of Gorebeck. In a prison in France I met a Captain James Frinton. We shared a cell for a week before I was moved. He is still incarcerated and has trusted me to deliver a message to his wife and daughter. He thinks you still live in Whitby but I managed to find your address from a stable lad.'

'Connor,' Lydia said, and smiled.

'Yes, your husband said that if I should return before he could I must please visit you and pass on his words. It would appear fate has indeed drawn us together.' He stood up and replaced the bed sheets carefully.

'All is for the best, in the best of all possible worlds,' Emma said quietly, quoting the words, hoping she remembered them accurately, from her father's copy of Voltaire.

'Candide!' he replied, and smiled at her. 'Some, I think would be naïve enough to believe that.'

4

Once the women had dressed they sat together around the square table in the cottage and broke their fast. The moist eyes of Lydia replaced the anger filled ones straight away.

The messages were of hope and love. He had also given Montgomery the name of an old family pet, and the name of 'Millie' that he always called his daughter. It was her middle one and favoured by her down-to-earth father; it had been a family joke that her mother and father called her by different titles. He also mentioned 'Socrates' with no explanation. However, it made Lydia laugh and then almost burst into tears. So it obviously had poignancy, with no given or needed explanation. None of this would be known to him if he had not met the man himself and known him as a trusted friend.

'How is he?' Lydia asked, as her daughter took hold of her hand. Both women's anxious eyes looked to him.

'He is quite well. There are negotiations taking place regarding a possible exchange. The only problem, is they seek a man who they presume has been captured by the British, an agent who works for Napoleon, who has been out of contact with them for some weeks. We are delaying negotiations because we cannot trace him.' Montgomery drank from his tankard and saw Lydia's expression change.

'You say 'we' as if you are working with the authorities.'

'Yes, I am. I have been sent by Horse Guards to trace this man, but because of what happened I was ordered by my superiors to attend a hearing. However, a message intercepted my journey, correctly coded, to carry on and ignore the hearing, so I made my way here. I trusted my cousin Gregory would listen and understand. I sought his help whilst I was in the region; however, I was to be greatly disappointed. I presumed the hearing would be cancelled by my superiors but I do not think word has reached Gregory. He believes I am a coward. Now my mission is more difficult by a tenfold.' Monty rubbed his head as if trying to clear his thoughts.

'So why not hand yourself in and explain? Surely all could be cleared up quickly,' Lydia questioned him. Emma could tell her mother was not at all sure about Montgomery's story.

'Because, before I could speak and make myself heard, I had been bound, kicked and near knocked unconscious.' He rolled back his sleeves showing the cuts to his wrists.

Lydia shook her head, she did not approve of such rough treatment. 'So how did you escape?' she asked, as she reached onto the shelf for the jar which contained some of her home-made balm.

'I feigned unconsciousness and was left unguarded for a few moments that is when I took to my heels. I managed to cut the ropes on a shovel in the stables and then ran through the woods to the ridge, gradually making my way down to the marshes and the shore. I knew this was Stangcliffe, Ebton or Seaham. Luck took my feet in the right direction or I would have perished.

'You must be made of strong stuff to have come all that way in your condition.' Lydia looked at Emma. 'What to do now?'

'I could try to get a message via the coach. I'd have to catch it at the top of Belton Bank; it may be possible as it slows for the descent,' Emma offered, but the look on both Monty's and her mother's faces told her this was not going to be an acceptable idea.

'No, miss. Although I appreciate the offer, it would be dangerous in more ways than one.' He rubbed the balm into his wrists, obviously enjoying the sensation and relief it gave.

'I need to travel back to London and clear my name. It is impossible to operate now that Gregory has raised such a fuss.' He looked more than a little annoyed.

'What if?' Emma began to speak with enthusiasm but was interrupted.

A knock on the door startled them.

'You best go in there,' Lydia gestured to the bedchamber. Without thinking Emma stood up too. 'Not you, my girl!' she added hastily, giving Emma a stern look.

Emma blushed but saw Monty wink at her as he disappeared from view, leaving the door slightly ajar.

A sharp gust greeted Lydia as she unlatched the door. Within seconds Annie Dilby had entered the cottage and slammed the door closed behind her.

'Ee, that's a mean wind today.' She beamed as she always did and proudly held out a freshly made loaf and a new apron. 'Tha apron is for the lass. I know folks down here haven't been too welcoming but I think a newly wed deserves a little bit of a gift to bring her luck. She'll no doubt need it!' She winked impishly at Lydia, and handed the apron over to Emma.

It was a sweet gesture from a sweet lady. 'Thank you, Annie, but I'm not . . .'

'Emma! Don't be rude. If a gift is well meant you should not refuse it. Now, go and get your Tommy out of his bed and tell him he has work to find. He may have served his King and country fine, but that isn't going to put food on our plates or in our bellies.' Lydia looked at Emma's ring finger and she quickly slipped it under the apron.

'Thank you,' Emma said, and blushed. She was now seen as a married woman. Her mother's warnings to her as a child of a little lie being like a small stone that turns into a boulder of untruth, never had such poignancy in her life before.

'That's alright; I know what it's like . . . I still remember, and soon enough you'll have a babe in that belly of yours to feed too. So you get that young man up and I'll tell my Bill that he will have another set of hands to muck out the stables, stack up the kegs at the inn, and slop out. It may not be much but I'm sure when folk see a man working hard they'll consider letting him go out on the boats and catch his share. But for now, he has to show what he is made of. So you send him over to the back of the inn and I'll tell Bill to give the lad, Tommy, a chance.' She nudged Lydia again with her elbow. ''E can always go up to the vicarage at Stangcliffe, the good Reverend has had gout bad for some weeks now and his missus is said to need a man about the place.' She laughed, winking and crude, but Lydia could find no harm in this woman, and smiled as she let her back out in the cold wind.

Then she turned around and leaned with both fists against the table, 'God help us, Emma!' she exclaimed, as Montgomery opened the door and looked at them both sheepishly. 'What a mess we've made of this whole situation!'

'I cannot thank you enough,' he said, but as both women looked at him, his words hung lame in the air between them.

'Word has flown around this hamlet quicker than the wind. Now everyone thinks that Emma is a newly wed and you are my son-in-law. If you do not appear at the inn, you will instantly raise suspicion and we will have the militia back here.' She stormed back into the bedroom.

Emma looked at Monty who stepped towards her. 'I can only say that I will put everything right. You two do not belong here. You could stay twenty years and you'd still be strangers. Trust me now, Emma, and I shall reward both of you and return your life to respectable society.'

'That's as may be, but Montgomery you are now 'Tommy'. My daughter would not be welcomed by any 'respectable' people if word of this farce reached their ears. Heavens, sir, if her father knew she had been in such close proximity to you it would not be the militia who would be a threat to your existence.' She shook her head, obviously flustered by events. 'Wear this,' she tossed him a jacket, 'roll up the sleeve a bit and they'll not know it's a bit short. Get yourself over to the inn, and wrap these around those wrists.' She passed him two pieces of leather. He realised they were wrist supports and he quickly placed them over the cuffs of his shirt, securing them.

'I'll not let yer down, Ma.' He smiled cheekily, and winked at Lydia.

'You had better not and you should remember to adopt that manner of speech. Don't go talking like you're an educated man. You are from . . . '

'Hull, it is a place I am familiar with, and have been a merchant seaman there, in my youth, before the war. So I should be able to pass any inquisition. I met your husband, and consequently yourselves, before I joined up. Injured out, but recovered enough to do manual work . . . chest you know

44

'. . . no good at sea . . . cough.'

'Don't get too sure of yourself, young man, but go, and quickly. Tonight we shall try to see a way out of this hole we have dug for ourselves. Until then, raise no suspicion. You arrived last night, troublesome journey or some such nonsense. Say the least, then there is less chance of making a mistake.' Lydia folded her arms and looked him up and down, nodding that he would do as he was.

He donned a woollen hat, arched his shoulders, and left.

Emma could not help but smile as he became his new persona and did as her mother bid. However, as her eyes fell upon Lydia's face, her good humour left her.

'How do we extricate ourselves from this? He needs to travel to London, or to find this man whom we can hand to the authorities and free your father.' She shook her head. 'This subterfuge is beyond me. I can't see how we can find out who it may be when the people are so wary of us. It could be a local man. It could be someone who was recently laid low.' Lydia raised and eyebrow.

'No Mother, if you're thinking of Mr Packman, I'm sure not. He loves his wife dearly.' Emma could not believe the coastguard was a spy. It was too far-fetched a notion.

'Who says spies can't fall in love? Anyone can.' Lydia stared at Emma.

Emma felt uneasy; she knew the words carried a warning against her developing any girlish infatuation with Montgomery. Well, Emma did not consider herself to be a girl and therefore dismissed the warning out of hand. 'We need to leave this place as soon as possible. Gossip is rife. Six weeks we have been here and, far from the friendly little hamlet we had hoped for, we have found only one person who will even communicate with us. That is a kind-hearted woman who is desperate for new faces to speak to and she is a meddling wife.' Emma looked down at her hands.

'This is our rented home. We cannot just move. Our home is also rented and we have to be careful with what coin we have. Have you any idea how much it would cost to travel and live in a larger town like York, Harrogate or London? Then there would be clothes needed, or we would be treated as trades people. Besides, now you are known as a wife of a ne'er do well who cannot hold down a decent job.' Lydia stared out of the window at the sea.

'Mother, there are many men who cannot find work so why would that be looked on in any way but with sympathy?' She folded the apron and put it in a drawer.

'You are naïve of the harshness of this world. He is a stranger. He is posing as your husband. If ever a situation was more ludicrous and dangerous I cannot think of one,' Lydia sighed, as she seated herself by the table.

'He knew Father.' Emma looked at her mother, and the lady nodded. 'Yes, there is no doubt they have met and that he trusted him,' she admitted.

'Socrates?' Emma sat opposite.

'He was a lover of truth. Your father said I should have been a politician, but he was glad I was not born a man.' She laughed and blushed at her memories.

'So are we to be just and seek the truth? Do we help Montgomery, or live here in a foolish lie, going nowhere?' Emma saw a glint in her mother's eyes. They had been dulled ever since the news had arrived that her father had been incarcerated.

'What do you suggest?' Lydia asked.

'He said he had worked on the merchant ships. Therefore he can handle a boat. We help him to go to Whitby where he can then get a ticket to the Thames.' Emma was filled with the excitement and audacity of what she was about to propose. 'But we go with him.'

5

'Tommy, lad, you get that back of yours into stacking these kegs against the far wall of the cellar. We have more arriving soon and I'll need the space cleared.' Bill's voice boomed down to him from the dispensary at the top of the cellar ladders.

The oil lamp flickered and Monty worked in the half light. It was good work to build up strength again whilst he had recovered from his ordeal. Monty had been working for the man for nearly two weeks. Despite Lydia and Emma's suggestion that they should get away from the area, Annie's interference had given him the opportunity he needed to try and infiltrate the locals, and therefore have an ear for whatever was happening. An inn was a good place to work quietly whilst listening to local banter and gossip. Superstition was rife in the place. Ignorance was king.

The militia did not come near the hamlet again. It was said they had abandoned their search presuming that the coward had done a runner and made his way to either Newcastle or Whitby. From either place it would be easy for a man to work a passage to London. There, any low-life could lose themselves in the Rookeries or Seven Dials.

Each evening he had taken out the bed roll from the cupboard, sleeping nightly by the fire in the cottage. Lydia kept a keen eye on him and Emma, which he found humorous at first, yet annoying as he would have liked to know Emma better. She had taken to wearing her grandmother's simple wedding ring and had found some work with Annie in the small bakery. They worked each day from early morning to late afternoon. He liked Emma, certainly he felt he owed her, she had saved his life and liberty, but it was her gentle humility that had touched him . . . and her understated beauty. Annie and her would go to market at the end of the week and sell the excess, bringing back more flour and supplies in return.

Lydia was not a happy lady. She missed her daughter's company and also was very nervous about the state of affairs they had found themselves in. Emma's future, to her, had been tainted, as if the lie would affect the rest of her life. They had to move from this hamlet before word spread to anyone who knew them. First, though, they had to help Montgomery find whoever it was that could be the agent. She had decided to visit the vicarage to try and find some work and information beyond the village. The three had agreed to work together. If by the end of the month they had not turned up anything of use, they would make their way to Whitby by boat, then London and on to Horseguards to try and sort out his and her husband's mess. He prayed that they could, for so far he only had dirt and sweat to show for his troubles.

'Okay, Bill, I'm nearly done. When do they deliver the next load?' Monty looked at the amount the man already held in store. He had no need of more barrels or kegs, which meant one thing. He was holding it for distribution, he was part of the free trade.

'Why do you want to know, man?'

'So I'll come back at the right time to help.' He waited for a reply but instead there was silence.

He finished stacking the kegs and then climbed the ladder. 'Bill, when do you want me back?' Monty stepped out onto the flagstones and replaced the trapdoor over the hatch.

Bill was leaning against the serving counter with his arms folded, and staring at him. 'Tommy, I'm not sure that I do.' He looked at him, with a strange stare.

'How do yer mean? Are yer not happy with my work? The lass will tear me off a strip if yer turn me down for

52

work, Bill. There is little enough to earn me keep around here.' Monty tried to look and sound sincere, edging towards desperate.

'Well, it's like this, man. I have business happening tonight that is not for strangers and folks with loose tongues. Business that can be costly — no I should say, deadly, to those who blab about it and I'm not sure I can trust you. So you see I have a dilemma.' Bill was a big man with arms that had the strength of a bear.

'You can trust me. I don't have anyone to tell nothing to. I only want to prove to my Emma that I can and will provide for her. She's married down, beneath her, if you understand me, and I want to come good for her so if her pa should return from the wars, then he'll not be disappointed.' He looked the man in the eye.

Bill thought for a moment. 'My Annie says that she trusted your Emma; even though she goes up to that coastguard's hut to feed his woman.

She says the old girl seems humble enough, despite being a bird who has fallen into our company from a loftier perch, but you, my man, you arrived here at night. You're fit and strong; funny that, and then the militia had been all over us like flies on a cesspit.'

Monty thought quickly, he trusted his gut reaction; it was time for a bit of a gamble. 'Look, that's why I was late arriving, but then they didn't get me, did they?'

'They said you was a coward, a deserter?' The man gave nothing away about what he was truly thinking. 'I don't hold with cowardice.'

'I'm no coward, Bill.' He stood straight. 'I'm a soldier, a good one, but I saw my friends slaughtered by the orders of a bad officer and I wasn't about to throw me own life away to appease some rich man's folly. I wanted to see my Emma again, and to raise a family. They don't listen to the rank and file; it's an officer's word that stands. Bill, I'm no coward!' He stood proud and faced the huge man square. It was with more than a little sigh of relief to Monty when Bill smiled back at him.

'So then, now we know little secrets, we have a reason to trust. I want you here just past midnight. No lights mind. We will be landing goods on the beach and need all the help we can to carry stuff. Give the old woman a sleeping draught and bring your missus to the shore. We will need absolute silence and swift helpful hands.' He patted Monty on the back. 'You'll earn more this night than you would in three months in the field.'

Monty nodded, smiled and made to walk past him, but Bill raised a strong hand and grabbed hold of Monty by the throat. 'Play me for a fool, man, and I'll rip out your tongue with my bare hands.'

Monty grabbed Bill's wrist and forced the hand away. He stared the man straight in the eye and repeated. 'I am no coward, Bill.' He released it and walked on.

'Then let's hope you're no fool, either.' Bill watched him go.

★ ★ ★

'You learn quickly, lass, don't yer?' Annie said, as she supervised Emma's efforts.

Emma took pride in what she was doing. It was true she wouldn't care to do this sort of thing day in and day out but she was fascinated by the process. She was actually doing work with her hands, and she found it hard but interesting. 'When do we go to market?'

'We take the small cart on Friday morn not long past dawn,' Annie answered, slamming a ball of dough down onto the table.

'Really, that early?' Emma could not contain her surprise.

'Aye, lass, or else we'll not get a good spot and not sell all our loaves. So you tell that Tommy of yours to let yer get some sleep.' Annie laughed, she was loud, rough and uneducated, but Emma loved the woman's good

56

humour and warmth. If not for Annie and Bill, they would be living in isolation from the other folk, who rarely spoke and resented them renting and moving into the biggest of the fishermen's cottages. Annie had provided an uneasy bridge between them and the villagers.

'So why was the militia so keen on catching your man then?' Annie asked as she calmly continued in her task.

Emma dropped the rolling pin and it clattered to the ground scattering flour everywhere. 'Oh, I'm so sorry, Annie. I'll clean it up.'

Emma flustered around until she could resume her work. Annie watched her and waited until she was calm again.

'Why, lass? Tell Annie the truth. She weren't born yesterday.' Annie leaned against the table to the side of Emma who was looking very nervous. 'They said as they were looking for a coward.'

'M . . . my Tommy is not a coward. He is brave and they had the wrong man.' Emma did not look up but tried to sound defensive of her 'husband'.

'Well, my Bill, likes him. So don't worry, we won't say nought. You best be careful though because if the other villagers twig to it, well let's say you're strangers and they aren't much trusted. We have been here nearly twenty three years and we are still outsiders. Mind, owning the inn gives us an edge, you might say.'

Emma set to her work, hoping she hadn't said too much.

'What do you know about the coastguard? His family are treated as outsiders also and he's been ill for his second month now.' Emma saw the mood on Annie change.

'Aye, well if he hadn't gone sticking his nose in where it weren't needed he wouldn't be ill now, would he?' Annie remarked as she kneaded the dough with renewed effort.

'But it is his job to, isn't it?' Emma asked.

'Lass, you have to wise up, love. Yes,

it was his job and the answer is simple — he should have chosen another one. People here are poor. There is little enough work. We have the sea and its harvest, but little else. If a man is taxed from every creature comfort whilst others with more pennies can enjoy an easy life, then if they find a way of putting food on their bairn's plates, they'll take it. Heaven help those who stand in their way.' Annie flipped the dough over and started working it again.

'But what if they're breaking the law and, in so doing, giving money to men in France — our enemies?'

'Lass, hush yer mouth. If you call free traders traitors they'll lynch you.'

Emma laughed. 'Well, then, they'd be murderers.'

Annie didn't respond in good humour as she normally would. 'Aye, they would be, so keep them thoughts to yerself.'

Emma paled a little as she looked at her friend, who just nodded at her. Both women continued working in silence, lost to their own thoughts.

* ★ ★ ★

Lydia walked up the steep road toward the headland of Stangcliffe. She was heading to the vicarage with a freshly baked pie and wearing a decent walking dress, coat and hat. She didn't want to be mistaken for a local, because she had decided to try to make an impression upon the reverend's good wife, whom she had heard was a mousy, yet educated woman. She knocked on the door with the large iron ring. The square, stark building looked like a mock up of a poor man's castle to Lydia.

A moment passed, then another. The wind blew and Lydia became impatient. She knocked again. No answer. She braved the wind head on and moved around the side of the grey building. It was exposed to the wind and the elements as it had been built at the top of the bank, at the base of the headland. From this vantage point the sweep of the bay was spread out before her but this was not the weather to stand and idly admire the view which spread on a clear day like today all the way to the Gannet Rock Light. It was as she skirted the back of the house that she saw a lady hanging out a sheet on a wash line. She was fighting to hang on to it and looked, to Lydia, as if she was near to tears. Lydia put down her basket and grabbed hold of the end which had broken free of the woman's grip.

Once it was fixed securely, she looked at Lydia as if she had appeared from nowhere. 'Thank you ... I ... am ... who are you?'

Lydia placed her hand upon her bonnet and gestured they stand out of the wind. She retrieved her basket and was shown to the back entrance of the house, which led to a scullery. Bedding was heaped in one corner, and tubs were filled with other towels and wrappings. The woman, thin and pale, looked near to dropping; Lydia felt a surge of pity for her.

'You'll have to excuse the mess, I'm in a bit of a fix. My housekeeper slipped and broke her leg last month and is now being cared for at her sister-in-laws over at Gorebeck. So I'm doing this myself and . . . ' The woman broke into tears; lost in an unfamiliar world.

'Come and sit down. I'll make us a nice hot drink and I'll help you sort this mess out. Here is a pie for dinner. Don't worry, when Lydia Finch offers to help out, things will become sorted.' Lydia heated the kettle and set about her work.

The lady followed what Lydia did and they started to make progress.

'Thank you, but what are you?' the good lady asked.

'A friend, I hope, but one that needs work for I have fallen on harder times. My husband, a captain of HM's Navy has been incarcerated in France, and my daughter . . . and husband and I have recently moved to Ebton.' Lydia placed a warm drink in front of her new friend.

'Well, we are both blessed by circumstance. You shall have the job of housekeeper until my Maisie returns, if you want it.' The woman smiled at her and a flush of colour returned to her cheeks.

'Very well, I accept,' Lydia smiled not believing how easy this had been.

'Then you shall return and fetch your things this day. I'll turn out a room for you and we can discuss your position when the Reverend has had his dinner this evening.'

'My things?' Lydia paled.

'Why yes, you would have to live here. You could not possibly trek there and back daily in all weathers.'

'But I have a daughter, you see,' Lydia explained.

'Who has a husband to look after her,' the lady reminded Lydia. 'There comes a time when we have to let our children grow up, Lydia. You won't be far away.'

Lydia could see the desperation in the woman's eyes. She thought of walking out there and then, but this was for her husband. She had to help free him. Two people in this household had been laid low recently. Could either be the spy? In the house she might be able to find out.

'Yes, we do,' Lydia said sipping her drink and feeling slightly sick inside. Could she trust Montgomery? Could she trust Emma, after watching her looking at him? She forced a smile; she would have to, because she wanted her man back.

6

Lydia walked slowly home. This was not the good news that she had hoped to take with her. It was not what she had planned. In her mind she had thought to befriend the woman, not work for her. How strange life was. Still, it would be temporary and she would be able to help James if she could find out if the Reverend was the man he sought. She found it hard to believe that young Packman was a traitor. He had nearly lost his life doing the job he believed in. It was all very frightening. So was the thought of leaving Emma. Her own mother would be turning in her grave at the thought of it. How would she explain to Emma that she was deserting her? How could she? This man was a stranger . . . yet he knew about Socrates, their secret and personal joke, and no one other than a trusted friend and confidante would have been given such a reference. She was supposed to return to the vicarage before nightfall. Lydia wrestled with her conscience. If she trusted Emma and she trusted Montgomery then what was the problem? Propriety need not know, after all, this was a desolate sort of place. That was why she chose it, perfect to hide away from all that had been before until James came home; he would, he must. What a mess her life was becoming!

* * *

Montgomery popped into the cottage shortly after Emma had finished work at the bakery. It would be an early start in the morning for her and she wanted a sound night's rest. She would go to Gorebeck and chatter to Annie on the way. Perhaps, she might say something which would be of use. Once Montgomery came home, she saw how happy he looked, and was certain that he had some news for her.

She smiled as he greeted her. It felt natural, yet strange, as if he had quickly become a part of the family. She was used to Annie calling him 'her man' and she found she had secretly grown to like the idea. Ebton had become to feel like a place that existed beyond her normality — unreal, detached from everything that was actually her life. Once they left its boundaries, Emma was sure things would change back to how they used to be; she would be Miss Emma Frinton, maiden, who had been away and had now returned to her home, and her father's care. Her mother would resume her usual form of dress and be busy organising something with the ladies of the town, and her father would be a captain once more, away for months then back with smiles, laughter and celebrations. She was certain that was how it would be.

'Now then 'wife', how has your day gone by?' He winked at her as he closed the door. He pulled back a chair and sat down at the table.

'Busy, 'husband',' she could feel her cheek flush a little as she said the word, 'but Annie is good company. She is suspicious about your sudden appearance here. There is little sympathy for Packman or his family. These people are dangerous, Tom . . . Monty. You should take great care. I think my plan would be better than staying amongst them. We could go to London with you. They are not looking for a man and his family, are they?'

'I have muscles. I know I have muscles, because every one of them aches.' He slumped forward.

Emma smiled, but felt that her comments were being deliberately ignored.

'You poor hard working soul.' She stood behind him, and rubbed both his shoulders with her thumbs and fingers as she had seen her mother do to her father after a long trip at sea.

'Oh that's nice.' He closed his eyes and smiled as he luxuriated in the feeling of her touch. 'Emma, I know this is awkward for you but we need to be here — I do. I'm sorry you have been compromised but I shall make all well again. I give you my word, Em. We need information to save your father. Give it another couple of weeks, then I shall take us to London.' He let his head flop back against her and looked up. Sparkling eyes and a broad grin adorned his face. 'I promise. Perhaps, it is your wish to come out in style, in the Season, hunt a beau who would never understand the gravitas and the bravery you have shown throughout your current situation. How you saved a soul and ended up in a sham of a marriage to rescue your fallen father. What secrets this maid will keep!' He winked at her.

She dug her fingers in a little hard and he flinched. 'Ow!'

'Serve you right! You have something of an impish child still in you, sir,' she remarked, and giggled when he opened his eyes wide at her, in mock shock.

The latch on the door lifted and

immediately Emma turned away to place the kettle over the fire. Monty stood up and walked to the jug of water by the small tub in the corner of the room where he could wash his face, neck and hands.

★ ★ ★

Lydia entered. She was very troubled, but as she looked at the back of one and then the other she thought to herself; good, they could not be further apart. Any attraction or growing fondness that she had thought to be there must have been all in her imagination. Perhaps they could make this work if she trusted them because, after all, Montgomery was a gentleman.

Emma turned to greet her mother. 'I was wondering where you had got to.' She smiled at her fondly and took the empty basket from Lydia's hand. As she did, Lydia's face froze mid expression; her eyes lowered and looked at the front of Emma's apron which was covered in dirt from the back of Monty's dust covered head.

'Annie appears to be lapse in her bakery. Is her flour really that colour?' She looked blankly at Emma, who glanced down and calmly shrugged.

'I must have caught it on the brush and pan when I swept the hearth. I shall have to take more care in future.' Emma turned away quickly.

'Indeed you will.' Lydia stared at the unswept hearth. 'Next time, remember to actually sweep the dirt up!' She snapped and walked into the bedchamber slamming the door behind her.

Emma looked at Monty and saw his guilty face break into a mischievous grin. She mouthed 'child' at him and they stared at each other, but neither could suppress the urge to smile.

'Emma!' The single word was a command for her to join her mother.

Emma almost jumped at the single word, her smile vanished and she entered the bedchamber.

'Shut the door behind you.' Lydia

was standing with her arms folded in front of her, looking extremely anxious. On the bed was her travel case, which was flung open.

'Are we going somewhere?' Emma asked. Suddenly her world felt threatened again. In that one moment she realised how much she liked this unreal world with her 'man' within it.

'Yes . . . well no . . . that is, I may be.' Lydia sat on the bed and placed her head in her hands.

Behind Emma, Montgomery had leaned against the door frame as Emma had not closed the door properly.

'What is wrong, Mrs Frinton? You only have to say if you wish me to leave, but I would not wish to abandon the two of you in this place. It is not safe and, if you will pardon my saying so, you were naïve in the extreme to have moved here.'

Emma saw her mother's face slowly look up at him as her back straightened. Emma braced herself for the tirade she expected to be unleashed from her mother. She was a woman who spoke out, and to have her judgement questioned in such a way was bold indeed, Emma thought.

Calmly and relatively quietly Lydia spoke. 'You may be both correct and incorrect at the same time. I was naïve. I did want to hide away until James returned and I wanted to be near the sea where I presumed he was, but despite the whims of an older woman, I may yet have found a way to help him. I have taken employment at the vicarage as their housekeeper. The Reverend has been laid low for some weeks. I aim to find out if he is the man the French want returned.'

'Mother, how can you be a house keeper?' Emma felt a strange panic growing within her. If they lived at the vicarage she would not be able to work at the bakery and follow the gossip, or visit the coastguard's family — or be with Montgomery.

'You do not think I have the skill?' Lydia looked abashed.

'No, not at all, but you are better than that, and besides, I cannot live there and still keep an eye on Packman or learn anything from Annie. How would I explain that 'Tommy' has been left to fend for himself?' Emma saw a strange expression on her mother's face, was it guilt, fear or suspicion?

'He wouldn't be,' Lydia replied, and stared fixedly at Montgomery.

'What you suggest is purely practical and may lead us to the right person, but it is dangerous and I am not sure you should become involved. There is a landing tonight of contraband, here on the beach. I do not want either of you to be there. What you do not know about you cannot speak about. It will happen at night time and I will be there. Between the three of us we can, in a much shorter time, find out the possible truth of what is happening here. I would prefer it if Emma could go with you.'

Lydia looked surprised. 'Would you, indeed?'

'Yes, I honestly would.' He stepped into the room.

'That cannot be. It would not be acceptable at the vicarage because they think my daughter lives with me and her husband. It would be extremely odd to the local people who already regard me with suspicion and . . . Emma may be safer with you.' Lydia could not look at her daughter, her eyes instead returned to considering the empty bag.

'You are seriously considering leaving me here? With Montgomery, posing as my husband?' Emma spoke the words but hardly believed this could be so.

'We need to help your father, Emma. But the question is, can I trust you two, together, alone? Temptation is an evil, who can disguise itself within woman or man.' She stared at Monty. 'Eve may have held out the apple but it was Adam who willingly bit into it.'

'Mother! What do you think of me?' Emma's cheeks and temper burned with indignation.

'I think you are a lovely, naïve

daughter that any mother would be proud of. I am a married woman, Emma, and it grieves me to put you in such a predicament. So, what of you, sir?' She stood up and looked at him.

'I am a man who would put his mission before more base thoughts. I respect your daughter and will protect her with my life if necessary. I owe her it already. This situation will not exist for long. By the end of the month I will return to Horse Guards and would ask you both to come to London with me and stay in my house, as guests. I am sure that you and my own mother would find a great deal in common, Lydia. For now, though, there is only trust that can take us forward.'

Lydia hugged Emma.

'I shall leave you two to sort out the bag and then take you to the vicarage. We can talk as we walk, Lydia. Meanwhile, Emma can sort herself out for her trip to Gorebeck tomorrow.'

Lydia sniffed. 'Yes, of course.' She turned around. 'Gorebeck is where the old housekeeper is, with her sister or some such. She had injured her leg. Might be worth inquiring about her, you could give her a message. Tell her that her mistress is fine, and has a temporary replacement.

7

Emma waved a tearful goodbye to Lydia as they started the walk up to the headland path. She had wanted to go with them but both said it would be better she stayed safe at home. Once she closed the door, Emma was surprised when her emotions changed. She looked at the little cottage that she had made into a home. She saw Montgomery's waistcoat, her father's cast off, over the back of the chair. She knew Eve was tempting her. It all seemed so natural to want him to be around, to talk and joke with her as he did, to have fun and to want so much more . . .

* * *

They walked beyond the fishermen's cottages, further than the inn and started to climb out of the bay. At first, neither Lydia nor Montgomery spoke, until they stood side by side looking down at a wild sea and the dishevelled row of buildings that made up this hamlet. There were an equal number of boats along the beach. What secrets did this place hide? Lydia asked herself. Then looking toward the church and the vicarage behind it, she asked herself the same question. Montgomery was staring beyond the sweep of the bay to the coastguard's house and the light at Gannett Rock. She thought he was wondering the same but then he looked down at her.

'I will take care of Emma. I have lived more of a worldly life than she has, which is why I would not endanger or compromise her. I respect her for all she has done for me. I owe that lady my life for rescuing me on the dunes and yourself for not turning me over to the militia. You shall both be rewarded and respected when I am through here.'

'So you say, sir, but do not think you

are in control in this place. We may all be deluded. Just . . . just behave with honour. Pressured times can make emotions highly . . . I mean, they can confuse and play tricks on a person, becoming unreal, stronger and more dangerous. Emma is so like her father, she will act before thinking. They are people of instinct and not forethought. They are precious and vulnerable because they will be taken in by the hapless soul, the underdog. They do not see lazy paupers in this world as some would judge the poor; they see lost souls and strays. They have good hearts, strong spirits and . . . '

He tilted his head on one side and smiled. 'Have a passion for life?'

Lydia sighed and poked his chest with her finger. 'Yes, a passion for life. Do not toy with me like you do my daughter, or I shall return with you forthwith!'

'I apologise,' he laughed. 'It is just that you are so fond of saying it is your husband that she takes after, yet I see you in her. She has your refinement, wit and intellect. I think she also has your passion for life and for justice, or else why did you hide me and at such a high risk to both of your reputations?'

Lydia could not answer. She had never thought of herself like her husband or daughter, as she was always the sensible one, but she knew in her heart he was correct. 'We must push on.'

'Indeed,' he said, and swung her bag slightly as he walked. 'Lydia, if you need me in a hurry, after dark, swing a lantern twice then count to five and swing it again. Repeat it up to four times. If I see it, I will come.'

'What if you don't?' Lydia asked.

'Then I won't unless someone else tells me,' he replied.

'That's a lot of help,' she muttered, and sniffed the cold air.

He chuckled and they chatted about her husband, until he left her at the vicarage gate.

'Take care, Lydia,' he said, and kissed

her forehead in what seemed a natural gesture.

'Take care of Emma and save your kisses for old women!' she snapped.

He winked at her and turned to leave. Lydia watched him and smiled. He'd make a fine son-in-law. She looked to the cross on the church and smiled. 'Please?'

She saw a movement by the kitchen window and made her way to her new position in life, determined to concentrate on what she was doing and not what Emma and Montgomery might be about to.

*　*　*

'Now, Emma, me dear, what's all this coming and going, eh?' Annie appeared at the door of the cottage. Emma instantly wished she had bolted it, but as usual she had forgotten to do so, lost to her thoughts as she was.

'Oh, Ma's decided to take the job of housekeeper that the vicar's wife offered her. She'll be living up there now for a while whilst her old housekeeper recovers. So it's just me and Tommy here.' Emma rolled up Monty's bed that was laid by the fire and pushed it into the cupboard. She wanted it to look like they were man and wife, or word would be around the fisher folk before Monty returned.

'You lucky, duck. When me and Bill were wed we had his ma and pa both living with us. What a bucket of fun, that was. Then when we had our Allan, Jimmy and Mark it just got more hectic and manic. Life is like that — all or nothin'.'

'I didn't know that you had children, Annie,' Emma asked, and instantly saw the sadness in the woman's eyes.

'Aye, I had more, but God took some for hisself. Now, there is Allan in the village, he is married with two little ones. Jimmy, he went to God in Nelson's great 'victory'.' Her words were bitter. 'Mark — well, the press got him, the bastards! I don't know when

I'll ever see my Marky again.' Unusually for Annie, she started to sob. Emma hugged her and the woman held on like she was a child. This was not the hardened wench the village saw; this was a woman grieving for all her lost little souls, her children.

'Look at me bleatin' like a bloody sheep. If my Bill could see me he'd knock some sense into my head.' Annie pulled away and took hold of the door latch.

'Don't go, Annie. Not like that. Have a drink with me and tell me about your boys.' Emma took out her father's best brandy and poured her a small glass.

'Now, lass, that's it. Now you're talking. This is good stuff.' Annie settled herself on the chair where Monty had sat only hours before.

'I don't want to talk about them really. I just miss all the ones not here any more. They were such good company when they were all here driving me mad with their antics. Now it's just me and Bill.' She chuckled,

'Mind we still have our moments but things change, lass. Life changes you. I used to be like you, once. Didn't know things then, and now some times, I wish that I still didn't.' She downed the rest of the brandy. 'Good stuff this.'

Emma poured her another one.

'Aye, you're a good lass. I was real shy when I met Bill. I was only just fourteen, but Pa decided that it was time I started a family of my own. He said Ma cosseted me.' She sniffed and Emma topped up her glass again.

'I've seen things that I shouldn't have. Even at that age, I had to 'help' and then I realised it was not the life Ma wanted for me, but Pa told me to keep quiet. He knew, you see, but Ma never let on.' She swigged the rest of the drink. 'You're lucky to have that mother of yours. She's a fine woman.' Annie stared at Emma a bit bleary of eye and Emma realised that she had already been drinking before she arrived. She was now very relaxed.

'What do you know, Annie, that is so

bad?' Emma placed a hand over Annie's rough one. 'Oh, here let me soothe those.' She reached up for her mother's balm and spent a few moments rubbing it gently into her chafed hands.

'Oh, that's good.' Annie closed her eyes and allowed herself to sink into the feeling of being soothed. 'It is best not to say, Emma. But don't go out to the beach tonight. There are landings going on. Don't let them see you or get you involved. Prison is no place for a lady like you. They'd break you, body and soul. Take care of that man of yours. Tell him, don't ask too many questions. They'd kill him. I've seen it done.' She shook her head and pulled her hand away. 'What am I rambling on about? You be ready in the mornin' and don't be late. We leave at first light.' Annie stumbled to the door. 'You should bolt this. Anyone could come in.' She left without closing it.

Emma did, as soon as she could. Annie had said she'd seen someone murdered! What kind of people did she

live amongst? The answer came immediately — murderers. She curled up in
her quilt awaiting 'Tommy's' return,
forgetting to put his bed roll back on
the floor.

8

Montgomery returned down the slope of the headland. He knew he was being watched. His time as a skirmisher had given him a sixth sense about such things. Walking through the village, deliberately slouching rather than striding out with his usual poise and gait, he made his way back to the company of his 'wife'. He had been born to gentry and had been groomed to stand tall, not to slump in posture, belittling his station in life. Expectation was that he would marry, produce sons and conserve the family wealth by marrying into equal or higher money. War changes things, perspectives, experiences and people. He thought of his home, his austere mother and then the warm smile of Emma, and knew which he would rather return to. All these thoughts didn't help him to discover the man who would end his mission and free Emma's father. If he, Montgomery, could do this it would reinstate his good name and leave a man indebted to him, one who would not be able to refuse him his daughter's hand, if he decided to ask for it, and of course — should she feel the same about him.

The small cottage at the end of the row looked dark and vulnerable, exposed to the open beach and the high tide. He wondered if that was how Emma felt, without the protection of her mother; the shutters were closed giving it the unlived in look. The shadow of the inn fell across it. He relaxed as the wind had abated slightly, but the noise of breakers broke the silence of the night. Montgomery tried to enter the cottage but the door was stuck firm, it had been latched. He knocked, not wanting to bring attention to the fact that he had been barred from his own 'home'. A nervous look upon Emma's face greeted him as she opened the door and Montgomery was let in.

'I had to bolt it,' she explained. 'I don't feel safe here on my own. He closed the door and secured it immediately and then turned and looked at her.

'Tell me, Emma, honestly, do you feel safe with just me here?' He leaned against the table and watched carefully for her reaction.

'Yes, but I do not know why I should.' A nervous smile crossed her face as she stared into his eyes.

His line of vision changed from her face to the floor by the fire — where the bed roll had been. He looked at her and raised a curious eyebrow.

Emma's face flushed slightly. 'Oh, no . . . I don't think you understand. I only put it away because Annie let herself in and I thought it would be best if I stopped her doing it again in case she found us doing something that would give us away. She wanted to know where you and mother were going. I'll fetch it back out now. I thought it would look odd if it was seen there because we are supposed to be man and wife.' She glanced at the fire, embarrassed and yet fighting an urge to smile or giggle, like a child.

'Emma.' He caught hold of her arm. Fearful eyes looked back at him. 'It is all right. I will see to it when I'm ready to sleep. Tonight I will be needed out there. You must stay within your room and not come out. It will be no business for an innocent young woman to be involved in. There could be the worst villains involved or just villagers making the best of an opportunity, but either way, knowledge of them and their ways is dangerous.' He moved towards her and slowly moved a curl of hair from her face. 'You have nothing to fear from me.' He lowered his head and kissed her forehead gently. 'I promise you . . . '

She pulled away from him. 'Monty, that is what I fear most of all.'

He chuckled. 'I seem to have missed something here, unless you have taken an innocent kiss as an advance toward something more.'

'No. Not at all . . . ' She lost the trait of what she was trying to say as she stared, lost, into his puzzled face.

'Was that supposed to make sense?' he asked.

'Yes, it does. It is because I feel so at ease with you that this situation is so . . . dangerous. It is as though I could start believing the lie is real.' She sat in a chair and smiled honestly at him.

He sat down opposite her still holding her hand. 'I feel the same way. Perhaps when we have sorted this mess out I should approach your father in a more formal manner. We could . . . '

The rapping noise upon the door broke the moment and Montgomery whisked Emma toward the bedchamber before he unlatched the door.

'Man, don't get comfortable and cosy like, because you are needed. Bill wants your muscle now. Fetch the wench, she can help us.' Josiah, an old fisherman with a weather worn face, glanced past him into the cottage as he sucked on his old clay pipe.

'She is not coming out this night. Tomorrow she will be going early to market and needs her rest.'

Montgomery grabbed his coat and closed the door behind him.

'You make a rod for your own back, man. You cannot let 'em get lazy. Bill will have Annie out lifting kegs,' Josiah snarled at him. 'Start as yer mean to go on, or they'll be soft and weak and demanding like.'

'I like Emma soft.' Montgomery smiled at the old man's look of disgust.

'Aye, until the novelty wears thin. Well, you'll have to do the work for two and get the pay of one. There's no fool like a young'un in love.' Josiah shook his head. 'Don't think Josiah can't remember what it felt like to take a wench for better or worse. I got the worse of it — what a tongue she nurtured as time's gone by, but I took her still,' he winked, 'I did, lad.'

* ★ ★

Emma tried to sleep but she couldn't. She heard Monty leave and was surprised how alone she felt. Her mother would be safe in a proper house and bed. Monty would be out in the wind and driving rain again, with wanton murderers by the sound of it, and she just couldn't sleep. Emma dressed and wrapped her shawl around her body. She did not feel safe, nor did she want to pretend nothing was happening. In her father's trunk, she knew, there was a pistol. Emma had seen him clean and load it several times before venturing out on a night or back to the ship. The streets around any harbour can be rough; it had been a habit with him. The shawl repeatedly caught on things so she dropped it onto the bed and took out one of his old jackets instead. She wore it with pride. Rolling the sleeves back, she felt strangely protected, as if something of him would keep her from harm. Placing the pistol on the table she set about preparing it. It was time, she decided, that this woman should protect her man.

9

'Mrs Frinton, if you would rise early — five o clock, I think, would be fine.' The woman looked around nervously as Lydia placed her possessions in the small chest of drawers next to the narrow single bed in the attic room. Her new 'mistress' was speaking to her from the top of the short flight of six wooden stairs which led up to the door to the room. She was propping the old rickety door open with her hand as it would otherwise have swung loosely shut. 'My husband likes the fires lit and the house warmed through on a morning. He hates the cold which seeps in overnight. He has a chest you know, it takes it badly.' She looked down and shook her head, the cloth cap waving about her sallow cheeks.

Lydia glanced down and saw her

shifting anxiously from one foot to the other.

'Then I think after you have prepared his tray — he likes his breakfast freshly cooked and hot, we should meet in the scullery and sort out the wash. I prefer poached rather than fried to break my fast, and a dish of tea. It refreshes me after a troubled sleep.' She sniffed, then continued as if just remembering the original conversation, 'I'm afraid those sheets . . . well, they're too much for someone of my disposition. I'm sure you'll cope admirably; you have a much stronger constitution than my own. Your life has prepared you for a hardier workload. I was always sheltered and have some education. I find some things difficult. More cultured and less practical, you could say.'

Lydia glared at her, thinking what else she could say, and wondering what foolish notion had brought her to take pity on this delicate butterfly, at her own constitution's expense.

The woman smiled genteelly at her.

'When you've unpacked meet me in the drawing room and I'll show you where things are kept.' The door swung shut as she scurried off. Lydia stared at the ill-fitting piece of wood as it swung on its hinge and pondered what sort of a mess she had landed herself in. If only her husband would return. That thought snapped her into action, as the sooner she could uncover something mysterious about this house on the headland or dismiss it, the sooner they might track down the man who would be instrumental in rescuing her dear captain and return him to their shores.

★   ★   ★

Bill shouted to Annie, 'Where's that helper of yours?'

'Oh, Bill, leave the lass in her bed. Young Tommy is working hard enough. I don't need no help down here.' She shouted up from the cellar where she was sorting contraband and transferring larger amounts into smaller vessels for collection or distribution. Speed was of the essence as they had to be clean away before first light.

'I tells yer . . . we're all in this or none of us. We can't have anyone with their hands left clean. I'll go and fetch her meself! They don't like foreign folk in these parts; we know that more than most so they have to muck in.' He disappeared from Annie's sight and with the speed and agility belying her build she was up the ladder in a trice.

'You'll do no such thing! You'd scare her to death and have young Tommy after splitting yer skull open. Make no trouble this night, Bill. We have important work to do. Tomorrow she'll be sat upon bales of silk and best leaf. There is no way the lass is not going to soil her hands too. But first let her do it without bothering her conscience. Once she's been a party to it, she can't say nowt, can she?' She winked as her Bill scratched his head.

'Aye, you're a sly one. I daresay that you know best but sometimes a sharp shock is necessary. If we have any nonsense from her, and her high and mighty ma, then I'll drag 'em out and you'll see who gets the wuppin . . . me or Tommy!'

'You calling me, Bill?' Monty appeared in the doorway with a keg balanced upon his shoulder.

'Aye, I'm callin' yer. Speed up man, we only have one night and you let that slip of a girl sleep like the dead, when she should be out of her cot and down there with my missus working.'

'I'll speed up. Keep Emma out of this.' Tommy stared at Bill who laughed at him openly.

'Set to work man and stop acting like a lovesick sop.' Bill took the keg from him and thrust his face into Tommy's. 'Remember, lad, I eat sprats like you for breakfast — Now speed up!'

Monty left the inn, plodding through the soft sand and heading to the breakers to unload the next batch. He was only just controlling his temper, determined to take Emma and Lydia far from this unholy place before the end of the week, before they were all arrested for smuggling or espionage or the murder of an arrogant inn owner, who Monty would gladly attack if he laid one hand on his . . . on his . . . Emma. He smiled as he waded into the shallows at the shoreline. 'On his wife!' he said out loud, but the sound of crashing waves took his words off into the wind.

10

Emma made sure that the cottage was in total darkness before slipping outside. She braced herself against the night air skirting close behind the building, crouching low, so that her progress would be hidden behind the stacked crab and lobster pots. The hung nets acted as a camouflage screen, billowing with each gust, as she ran across the open sandy track and up onto the nab, behind the inn. She was careful to lean low so that she would not be seen as a silhouette on the horizon. Once there, she huddled behind one lonely gorse bush. It offered little shelter, but she could make out the figures as they moved around the beach ferrying the goods from the white breaking surf to the dimly lit inn.

Looking to the headland she saw a low light flicker — or thought she had, but was not sure if it was a trick of the night. At the other end of the vast bay the distant light of Gannet Rock occasioned a distant flare across a turbulent sea. It was too far for her to see if there was any movement within the coastguard cottage.

The small hamlet of fishermen's cottages was static except for the odd ghostly figure that darted in between. In the dark they looked ominously like the harbingers of death. Emma waited; she watched a figure skirt their cottage. In the dim light she could not make out if it was male or female. Tall or short, just a hunched blurred image but there was no mistaking their intent, as they slipped inside her adopted home. Emma could not help herself recoil in fear. She should have been in there, asleep and oblivious to all that was happening around her. Instead, like an owl, she watched, but lacked wisdom as to know what to do next. What if it was Monty? Would he panic and think she had been abducted? Worse still, what if it was an abductor? She was frozen with indecision. What should she do? Stay where she was, in the open, or return and face whoever was in her home? She thought of her father — what would he do? She asked herself. The answer came to her in an instant. It was the advice he had given her repeatedly throughout her life — follow your instinct, girl. With her hand on her pistol, she was determined to do just that.

* * *

Lydia saw to her immediate tasks of making up a tray for her new 'master', strange as it seemed to be making anything for anyone other than her beloved James. Yet, she was fascinated and surprised by the Reverend Brampton and his wife. She had not been introduced to the man. In fact, she had not heard nor seen him since arriving. The evidence of an invalid in the house was all apparent in the scullery, but the house was as quiet as the dead. She shivered as she thought the unfortunate phrase. Perhaps it was better not to think in such a fashion.

In the scullery, the lady of the house soon joined her. Lydia was looking with distaste at the mess the woman had let things get into.

'I thought if you began by sorting the sheets first, starting with boiling the most soiled ones first, and then seeing to the lighter stains and smaller towels and nightshirts next . . . ' The woman looked at Lydia as she placed both hands defiantly on her hips.

'You did, did you?' Lydia replied. 'Did it take you long to think this?'

'I do not care for your tone, Mrs Frinton. Yes, it did take me a while as I had to consider the priorities, and in emergencies we have to swap duties around. I shall help with some of the meal preparation to ease your load whilst you catch up with the backlog of washing. It will be all part of your duties. I have drawn up a list and have agreed with my husband a suitable remuneration paid at the end of each month when you will be granted a full day's leave.'

'Mrs Brampton,' Lydia's voice was quite loud and her manner direct, 'I offered to take the position of 'house-keeper', to help you, in a moment of charity. You seemed so helpless . . . hapless even. In no circumstance did I agree to come all the way up onto this Godforsaken place to become a scullery maid or general dogsbody!' Lydia glared with indignation as she spoke.

The woman trembled slightly, visibly cringing when her home was likened to a place where God was absent. 'We have no scullery maid. We have no other servants . . . I just cannot cope alone. I don't know how, you see. When Maisie hurt her leg and left, I was desperate. I thought you'd cope, just like she did.' She looked abashed, but this time Lydia refused to be moved.

'Then, may I suggest you learn how to, and quickly. You are a married woman of the world and it is about time that you did, I think. Perhaps we could employ the services of a village girl for a week to catch up, and then see if she may be needed for a day every other week beyond that.' Lydia tried to offer a solution that was more practical than her storming out in a temper.

'Oh no, my husband would never agree to it. He is a man of thrift.' Mrs Brampton looked down at the sheets. 'Besides, he does not like strangers around his home when he can not 'guide' them through life's path. He needs to know they are of good character and sound heart.' She smiled shyly, admiration of her husband's foibles obvious for Lydia to see.

'Then let him wash the sheets himself.' Lydia folded her arms. 'Perhaps it is time I met him and we had a chat about my proposed employment. He has not, as yet, encountered my heart, or my head for that matter.'

'Tomorrow will be soon enough. He will be resting now.' Her eyes were almost pleading with Lydia not to push the point.

'Very well,' Lydia remarked, almost casually. 'Pick up that bundle of soiled linen and place it in the hot tub, then fill it with water. I shall set to soaking some of these and between us we shall regain some order. Then you will send word to the village that you urgently need a scullery maid for a week's work. If anyone comes forward, we shall keep an eye on them and set them to a hard day's graft from 6am to 10 at night. No idle hands or tongues for mischief then.' Lydia raised an eyebrow, but Mrs Brampton did not contradict her.

'Perhaps your daughter would like to help.'

'My daughter will not be working as a scullery maid for anyone — ever!' Lydia almost rounded on the thin-framed woman; her rage almost palpable.

Quickly she picked up a bundle of sheets and clumsily rolled it into the large hot tub that was on a ledge next to the scullery fire. 'I was only thinking aloud.'

'Then don't! It is not an acceptable position for my Emma,' she explained.

'Isn't she a fisherman's wife?' Mrs Beesworthy looked genuinely puzzled. 'You will call me, Ma'am, though, or by my title. I shall not be made a fool of in front of the hired help.'

Lydia chuckled. 'No, Ma'am, but you will treat this lady,' she pointed to herself, 'with respect. I am Mrs Lydia Frinton and I am no one's hired help unless it suits me to be so and my daughter is not going to slave away for you or anyone. Is that clear?'

'Quite,' the woman replied through thin lips. However, she set silently to her task.

*   *   *

'Tommy, when you've finished with those kegs, get yourself back to your lass. She will no doubt be feelin' a cold draft down your side of the bed. Best go warm yerself up a bit. You've done well, lad. You're used to hard work and that bodes well with me.' Bill tossed him a small pouch with coins in.

Monty smiled as he felt the weight of it. 'Thanks, I will.' He climbed the ladder out of the cellar and saw a very weary Annie saying goodnight to her husband.

'Get to bed, woman, you'll have four hours kip before yer up and at 'em again.'

'Night, Tommy.' Annie winked at him. 'Make sure that lass of yours is up good an' early. I can't wait. We have to set our stall up for the first customers or we'll miss the trade and our contacts.'

'She'll be there,' he said and smiled before thanking Bill one last time for his cut. It was only as he approached the cottage door that he felt something might be slightly amiss. The activity of the previous hours had ceased. Shadowy figures had blended into the night. The only evidence of what had been happening was written in the damp sand — tracks that would soon be washed away by the sea, hidden forever.

Monty pushed the door open with one finger, carefully standing to the side in case he should be attacked. Old habits from the army were hard to pass over. He and his men had usually been skirmish troops going on ahead, testing the lay of the land. It was a position he had enjoyed as he felt his heart pound, trying to outwit a resourceful and cunning enemy.

The door had been left ajar. There was a low fire burning in the hearth; next to it, smoking a clay pipe was seated a cloaked figure.

'Come in out of the cold, Montgomery Wild, before we have a welcome committee to greet us formally.'

Monty showed himself in the doorway. He stepped inside and carefully closed the door behind him. Glancing at the bedroom door he spoke, 'What do you want Gregory? If it is my skin, why did you not send your rabble down here?'

'We are quite alone, Montgomery.' The man drew a long draft on his pipe. 'There is no reason we cannot have a civilised conversation here undisturbed by your new-found friends.'

Montgomery flung the door of the bedroom open and saw the empty bed, the night-gown folded neatly upon the pillow. 'What have you done, Gregory?' He stepped towards him, but then heard the click of his cousin's pistol.

'Calm down, Monty. I've known you were here all along. Although,' he chuckled, 'I must admit you have provided yourself with very comfortable homely surroundings. It was quite easy to slip in here when all hands are involved in such illegal affairs. Surprising really, you would suspect that it would be the opposite case. The locals must be getting complacent.'

'When you arrived, Gregory, was there no one here already?' Monty asked, trying not to show the concern he felt, in his voice.

'Obviously not, or there would have been a fight, man.' He smiled. 'And that would have brought my men down in numbers which would have ended in more than one villager being hurt, I assure you.'

'What game are you playing? Why not make arrests if that is what you are about, or have you seen light of day, and realise I am an innocent man?'

'Oh, that you are not, my man. You are now a smuggler. I could have you destroyed or transported.'

Montgomery looked at him. 'So why do you not?'

'Because, cousin, you are more use to me here.'

11

Gregory placed his pistol carefully on the table, still pointed toward Monty. 'Come, let us talk openly. I have received news that you have been exonerated from charges laid against you. In fact, you are to be commended for bravery when you return to Horse Guards. I salute you, sir.' He flicked the rim of his hat, in a carefree manner.

'So why set your hounds on me to the point of giving me a thrashing and threatening me within an inch of my life?' Monty leaned against the wall, his arms folded. He needed to focus on the current situation, but was distracted with concern over where Emma had vanished to.

'Monty, you were running away from my men. They thought they were tracking a traitor and a coward. What would you expect?' He shrugged his shoulders.

'I would expect you to know me better, Gregory. Was it not I who always rescued you from the tree when you climbed too high?' He glanced to the hook by the door and saw that Emma's shawl was still upon it. She cannot have gone far. He wondered if, perhaps, Annie had given in to Bill's wishes and fetched her for work stashing goods over at the bakery.

'Yes . . . you were always the hero. Things haven't changed much, or have they? Now you appear to be in the company of rogues. You land, hide and peddle contraband. How low the hero has stooped. You have swapped the company of gentlemen and ladies for the hovel in which you hide out with whores and thieves.' Gregory's mouth was set firm.

'There are no whores living under this roof, sir.' Monty stood straight. He saw the glint in Gregory's eyes and knew instantly that he had reacted as the man had hoped he would. It was a triumph as his cousin had needled him deeply; the glint was not due to the reflection of the flickering flame within the fire.

'So are you actually wed to the girl then? I hear you have a 'wife'.' He sat back enjoying his moment.

'It is not as you think.' Monty looked to the door; where on earth was she?

'Are you wed?'

'No, of course not! Get to the point of this charade, man!' Monty was trying hard to control his temper.

'Then whore by any other name, she must be,' Gregory drew on his pipe.

Monty took a quick step toward him, he would not stand by and have Emma derided by his smug cousin, but the pistol was swiftly lifted and aimed at him again, with his free hand. 'Don't be a fool. She is irrelevant. Why have you stayed here? Do you have your man, yet? Do you know who it is yet?' Gregory placed the gun back down as Monty stepped back.

'I have my suspicions but no proof.'

'Then you and I must collude. I have

suspected the coastguard for months. When word came that the messages had stopped and they wanted me to turn over the traitor, it all seemed to fit. Yet, I have their house watched day and night and no attempt at sending or receiving a message has been traced. I dismiss him now because he would be too obvious. What better position to be in to pass on secrets and move freely around the coast, than that of coastguard. No, it is too obvious and therefore too easy for him to be the man. Besides, I believe him to be an honourable, if not unlucky young man.' Gregory sighed, 'Which leaves me with a blank sheet again.'

'Who else would be placed with the knowledge and opportunity to pass it on? I agree with your deduction, but there has to be a realistic alternative.' Monty looked at him. 'So who else?'

'I do not know. I have also had the vicarage watched, and the same applies except for the older member of your little harem who appears to have found employment there, no one new has come or gone from the house in as many weeks.' He shrugged. 'Monty, I have to find them . . . my position is being questioned. I even wonder if they suspect me.'

He was looking pointedly at Montgomery.

'You had crossed my mind. You have the position and the opportunity and you would have been warned off some weeks ago that someone was onto you. So, what better way to cover your own tracks than to catch a scapegoat?' Monty held his gaze.

'You thought I had chosen you to be it?' He chuckled. 'What a trusting family we are.' He spun the pistol around so that the barrel pointed to him. 'Go on then, arrest me if you truly believe that.'

'Put it away, man, before it goes off and you shoot yourself in the foot — as you are apt to do.'

Gregory smiled. 'I need your help.'

'Then, perhaps it is because of the

watch that they have ceased the activity. Remove your men from the headland and see if anything happens. If not, then do so for the coastguard's house. It is the only way we will know if an opportunity that we give will be taken, for whoever it is who would take it. Leave here quietly, Gregory, unseen or else you will forfeit not only your own life but also mine and the respectable young lady who has helped me thus far.'

Gregory stood up and held the pistol at his side as he approached the door. Monty stepped in front of him. 'I will speak to you at the manor, by the end of this week. If I need help, will your men be ready to back me up?'

'Of course, Monty — for King and country!' he whispered, and smiled before slipping out into the darkness of the night. Monty watched him through the crack as he left the door slightly ajar. He made his way along the beach avoiding the village and then cut through the dunes and marshes. Monty was about to search for Emma when he saw a figure follow Gregory into the dunes. Quick as a shot Monty followed, keeping his head low and his wits sharp, all the while wondering where Emma was. He had to find her before day dawned and she was missed. He could hardly say he had misplaced his wife.

★ ★ ★

Emma waited until the figure re-emerged from the cottage. She had been prepared to rush in if she thought that Monty was in any danger, but as she crept back down to the cottage she heard most of their conversation. When Gregory was about to leave she scurried behind the building and waited for him to make his way up the bank. He did not do this, so she followed, curious as to where he was going. She did not trust the man and was determined to protect Monty from any man who was so coarse and would call her a 'whore'.

Once in the dunes she heard voices.

She crawled on her belly until her head was hidden by the long wiry grass which held the sand together in the form of hillocks. Glancing down into the valley between the crests she saw two shadowy figures, one holding the reins of a horse.

'Well, does he know?' the stranger asked.

'No, not even close.' Gregory took the reins.

'What to do then?'

'Wait until he does. Watch him, closely,' Gregory said, in a barely audible tone and mounted.

'Aye, I'll do that. What of the wench? When he's done with her, she'll need a man. I might make an arrangement myself,' the stranger said.

Gregory rode off.

The other figure darted between the dunes. Emma was ready to slide down the steep sandy slope of the dune when someone grabbed her by the waist of her father's coat and flipped her over.

She punched low as she turned, and was rewarded by the figure bending double over her and cursing. She was ready to bring the pistol down on his skull when she saw it was Monty.

'Damn you, woman!' he spluttered, as he straightened.

'You fool! I nearly had him. I nearly found out who it was that your cousin met!' she whispered.

'Did you? What if he had found you? You know what they think you are?' Monty crouched over her, keeping a low profile so as not to be seen.

'Well, is it any wonder when you rest on me so?' Emma said indignantly.

'Woman, I am trying to save you,' he reasoned.

'From what?'

'Yourself,' he said, and kissed her lips lightly before easing his weight from her and disappearing down the side of the dune to follow the stranger's tracks.

★ ★ ★

Lydia rose early, as she had been requested to, but more for her own peace of mind than anything. As day dawned she looked over the bay; she could see fishing boats making their way out into the open sea. The village was a hive of activity with women and children seeing to their daily chores. A wagon was being pulled up Belton Bank to the moor road. She thought she could just make out Annie driving it. Although she stared hard, try as she might, she could not see sign of Emma. How she missed her daughter. They had never been separated for more than a day and the girl's absence made her ache inside. Deciding emotion would be a waste of her energy, she returned to her chores and went down to the kitchen to prepare the Reverend's tray.

Once ready, she carried it up the servants' stairs to the main landing and made for the Reverend's room.

His wife greeted her. 'Thank you, Lyddy. I shall take it from here.'

'It is not necessary. If you open the door I shall set it on the table for you.' She smiled at the woman. 'My name, by the way, is Lydia.'

Mrs Brampton took hold of the tray and pulled it firmly from Lydia's hands. 'I shall take my husband's tray in and when he is ready I shall present you to him. Please send word to the village that we need a scullery maid for a few days.'

'Very well,' Lydia said, and turned back the way she had come. Before descending the stairs once more she glanced back and saw the woman place the tray on the carpet. She unlocked the door of a bed chamber and then picked up the tray. Before entering the room she smiled brightly and greeted her husband with a hearty 'Good morning, my dear,' promptly shutting the door firmly behind her.

Lydia thought she was a very odd person and was glad to wrap her shawl around herself and set off to the village with her message, hoping that she would see Emma safe and well, whilst she was there. When she glanced up at the house she could have sworn she saw a curtain move in one of the upstairs rooms but, when she brushed a hair from her eyes and looked again there was Mrs Brampton hanging out some smaller items on the wash line. She gestured to Lydia to hurry, and so she went on her way as quickly as the wind and rickety path would let her.

★　★　★

Monty scrambled over the dune but the trail was lost as the sand gave way to the wild grass and marsh. It was too dark to risk following into the marsh paths unless he was familiar with the lay of the land. Defeated he returned to Emma, as she made her way behind him.

'You lost him?' she said, as she regained her posture, standing in her father's heavy coat.

'We did,' he replied.

'Well if you'd let me go after him and not dragged me down, I would have . . .'

'You would have been lost at night amongst marshes, with strange men afoot. No, Emma, you can not continue in such cavalier fashion. We must return to the cottage and you shall make ready for your trip to Gorebeck with Annie. I shall check things are still right with your mother as soon as light dawns.

12

Emma sat, by Monty's side as he crouched over the rolled out mattress and neatened its edges.

'All ship shape,' she said and smiled at his handiwork.

'Spoken like a true Captain's daughter.' He placed a comforting hand upon her shoulder. 'We will get him back. If Gregory has reason to dismiss the coastguard then we must look to the headland. The Reverend has not been seen for nearly six weeks. Then the housekeeper mysteriously disappeared after an accident. Perhaps you can trace her whilst you are in Gorebck. She is Mrs Maisie Ashton, you can tell her your mother is helping out at the vicarage. That gives you a legitimate reason to enquire after her whereabouts, but take care. I shall not be there to look over your shoulder, and see you safe.

'How do you know you can trust Gregory?' she asked, liking the feeling of security his touch and words gave her.

'I don't, but we have little enough else to go on. After all, he found his way in here to speak to me. How else could he have done it, or would have done it, if he did not know something about the village, their doings and my presence?'

She stood up. 'If he was involved in some way in the trade or if he had a contact here, then it would explain how easily he moved through the village. There were others about, I saw them, from the nab. However, not the man he met, yet he spoke well, was strong and worked for him. He doesn't know we saw him, but that man does not look or sound like any man here. So who was he? How did the villagers not know they were both here? It is all very disconcerting.' She rubbed her eyes, feeling very tired.

He took her father's coat from her shoulders and placed it on the table.

'Take care,' she said. 'I had the pistol in the pocket.'

He pulled the weapon out of the back of his belt. 'You should always know where your weapon is; if not, please do not carry one.'

'I was going to protect you,' she said defensively.

Montgomery did not laugh at her, but placed a hand on each of her shoulders and pulled her gently towards him. 'It is I who should be protecting you, Emma.' He held her close before bending down and kissing her lips, tenderly at first. Emma felt a growing urgency within him and responded to it. She had dared to dream of such a moment, hoping that it would occur spontaneously, like this, and so was more than ready to respond. Both were filled with a mutual passion and desire, but it was cut short as abruptly he stepped away. Turning his back slightly to her, he ran his fingers through his hair then looked back more than a little sheepishly.

'Did I . . . have I done something wrong?' she asked, puzzled and slightly hurt by what would appear to be his rebuff.

He laughed and then apologised. 'No, Emma, you did everything just right . . . believe me. I promised your mother that she could trust me and I must be strong. Forgive me, I should have known better, but I will not let my feelings for you be the cause of your ruin. We must extricate ourselves from this mess safely, then Emma, I promise I will honour those intentions. Then will be our time, not now.' He took her hand and kissed the back of it. 'Until then, you must catch what sleep you can before Annie arrives for you to go to market.'

Emma blushed, she was tired, happy and, if she were honest, swept with a surge of disappointment that for once in her life she had not been allowed to throw caution and propriety to the wind. She saw before her a man she wanted, and she knew nothing would stand between her having him. 'I shall track down this Maisie, and you must promise to make sure that mother is safe. If Gregory is right she could be in danger.'

'I will, I promise.' He watched her go to the bed chamber and sighed. He had done the right thing . . . he had. As he crawled into his own bed by the hearth, he was still trying to convince himself.

★ ★ ★

'Lass, you look half dead! And you're allowed to sleep nights. You'll have to toughen up. Go lie in the wagon and I'll get us to market. You'll have another hour at least. Is that man of yours too demanding?'

Emma blushed, she didn't know how to reply so climbed onto the wagon amongst all Annie's goods and atop what she suspected was a layer of contraband. If her father could see her now, she thought, but then felt sad as she wished he only could.

'Well, lass, you're going to have to say no to him and mean it. You have to set 'em right or you'll not have a say on nowt. Now me and Bill, we sorted it out long since. We know where we stand and . . . ' Annie's voice drifted on and on but Emma soon fell asleep, thinking of Monty and wondering how it was that Gregory had slipped into the village so easily. Annie said they had lookouts to all the roads and moor trods, so how could he have found a way in, undisturbed. It bothered her.

Lydia arrived at the cottage early and caught Monty before he set off to the inn.

'Has Emma gone?' she asked, and quickly looked around. He had been putting his roll back in the cupboard when he let her in.

Lydia made no pretension of hiding her feelings or concerns as she quickly checked both rooms. 'They need a chambermaid up at the hall. His sheets have been piled up for a week or more and the woman is useless.' Once she had made her assessment of the situation she actually looked Monty in the eye.

He smiled at her. 'Would you like a warm drink before you head off back? I'll ask at the inn for you. Bill will know if there is a girl needing work around these parts.'

Lydia sat down and nodded. 'This isn't easy, Montgomery.'

'I know, but have you seen the Reverend yet?' he asked as he gave her a drink to warm and calm her.

'No, I can't get into the room, but I will. There is something strange about the place. The woman seems so helpless, and yet she is strong when it comes to guarding her husband. I can't make it out.'

'See if you can. I want to know if he is tall, well spoken and quite well.' Monty explained that Gregory had met such a man. It did not make any sense to him but nevertheless he would find out if there was a connection between the two.

'If your cousin found his way here, then he knows that you and my daughter are pretending to be married. He is a member of society. Her name will be forever sullied by this. Whatever do I tell her father when he returns? His freedom will have come at a high price, sir.' Lydia looked at him; her heart was troubled and heavy.

He leaned forward and looked straight into her eyes. 'I give you my word, Lydia, your daughter will not be harmed by this. I have strong affection for her and I intend to make our current fictitious situation into a reality.' He leaned back as Lydia's face showed some relief.

'But we know so little about you. Are you a man of means, or a cad? A good catch, or a philanderer?' She watched his face, his expression serious.

'No you don't, but until this matter is resolved, you will not. Lydia, like your daughter you shall have to trust me. Then, and only then shall I reveal all.' He winked at her. 'I am late. I have my wife to feed, so I must earn my keep. Find out by Friday what you can, then we leave on the tide, and I want both of you with me. This mess is becoming too dangerous.'

'But what of my husband?' Lydia stood up.

'I think I am beginning to understand what is happening, but for now, carry on as the housekeeper. I need you to see inside the Reverend's room.'

13

Emma woke up with a jolt as Annie slapped her leg. 'If you've done sleeping, missus, perhaps you could move yourself and give me a hand.'

Emma climbed out of the back of the wagon and found herself in a town square behind the local church. It was, she thought, a pretty place with a bridge over a river, where roads from north, south, east and west met. This was Gorebeck, a busy, growing market town.

Annie set to with her table and had Emma place the baking upon it. It felt as though it was still the middle of the night as daylight had barely broken. You stay here, lass, and serve and I shall take the wagon around the inn for stabling. Emma looked at the back of the vehicle, slightly puzzled.

'But we haven't unloaded everything

yet, Annie,' she said as Annie dropped the cover back over the drab coloured wagon and glared at Emma.

'You be about your business, lass, and I'll be about mine!' Annie climbed back up and drove the wagon towards the inn. Emma was left to sell their produce for the meagre amount it brought in. She realised that Annie's other business would be far more lucrative.

★　★　★

Lydia, with the help of Montgomery, managed to find a young woman in Ebton who was not too bright, but she was very strong and keen to work in the big house. Her family were more than willing for her to earn some extra coin for a week and Lydia was pleased that she had extra hands to take the bulk of the scullery work from her. The girl was soon ensconced in her tasks which meant Lydia had time to see to her chores in the main house.

'He sure bled enough for a man with

leg problems,' Biddy said, without thinking more on it.

However, Lydia did. The girl had innocently stumbled upon a simple observation which had passed Lydia by. She knew she had to see what had happened to the man upstairs.

Mrs Brampton joined them fleetingly to give Biddy a cursory talk about what was expected from her and at what remuneration. She seemed satisfied and then turned to Lydia.

'The key to the linen cupboard is always kept on a peg in your room; it was, of course, Maisie's room and she was a trusted employee. We expect our employees to be beyond question as to their morals. Make sure that all of these sheets are piled neatly within the cupboard once they are clean and pressed. I don't like scullery maids entering the main house, so that is your duty, Lydia.' She was brusque in her manner; again, Lydia thought, she was trying to establish her authority over her. This time Lydia let it pass because she wanted to be in the main house, and was determined to enter the Reverend's room. Montgomery had given her a description and she would see if he fit it. It was not unusual for the local clergy to be involved within, or have knowledge of, the trade, but to be involved in espionage was treason and that was something else.

'I shall go and make sure all is in order and, if not, make some space, Mrs Brampton.' Lydia saw the woman nod at her, as if she was satisfied with her attitude and was happy for her to leave, whilst she gave further instructions to the young Biddy.

Lydia was quick to find the key. The linen cupboard was situated on the upper landing. She saw to her task quickly, then quietly made her way along the corridor to the Reverend's bedchamber. She placed an apprehensive hand upon the door knob and slowly started to turn it. Carefully it moved, silently she continued until the lock was unlatched.

She glanced over her shoulder to see if Mrs Brampton was coming. The door to the house opened and closed. Lydia breathed slowly out, as now the woman would have gone for her morning walk. The door had been kept locked, but on occasion, like today, when the woman was preoccupied, she forgot. The door was now ajar. Lydia walked calmly into the room, and froze.

★ ★ ★

Monty was working in the cellar at the inn; it was hard work but he often heard conversations from the room above. He was busy listening to old Amos talking about the movement of the militia in the night; he thought he'd seen them hiding in the gill, and wondering why they didn't come down upon the landing. So he thought they were either cowards or being paid. Either way it wouldn't lose him sleep or stop him drinking. Monty was so engrossed in listening to this that when Bill appeared behind him he was taken by surprise.

'Where is that lass of yours . . . Tommy?' He was leaning against the cellar wall, his arms folded in front of him.

'She is in Gorebeck with Annie,' Monty looked up at him, 'you should know that.' He was surprised by the question. For a large man . . . a tall man, he was light of foot. Monty had not heard or seen him climb down the stairs. Bill's stance was more upright than usual and the voice was less accented. 'Where was she last night then?' He stared at Monty.

'Until the early hours, sleeping, then your lass came and got her. She was in the back of the wagon when they left.' He moved the last keg into place then stood straight. 'Why do you ask?'

'Because she wasn't in the cottage last night, was she?' His arms dropped casually down to his sides.

'Now then, how would you know that?' Monty asked, and stepped toward the ladder.

Bill raised his arm and placed it across Monty's path, blocking him from climbing up the steps. 'I know everything around here, Mr Montgomery Wild, and I am watching you closely. Keep your mouth shut about what you've seen here to your superiors in the smoke, or I'll close it permanent, like. Look at what happened to that young coastguard. You keep that cousin of yours out of my hamlet or I'll see he doesn't visit here anymore. We have a cosy arrangement and I don't want him breaking anyone's trust, or pushing his luck. Take your women out of here and go . . . soon. You don't belong . . . none of you do.' Bill was almost breathing into his face he was so close, intimidating.

'I intend to, William,' he glanced at the man's arm, 'so if you are not working for him, then what business do you have in common?'

'Don't get clever with me, man. I don't want any business with the vermin, but he caught one of my men and they told him things. Then he talks to me about traitors, and I don't hold with that. So he now has a cut of the goods and I can operate with ease, and we work together . . . until the traitor is caught.' He moved his arm.

'What then?' Monty asked.

'Then, we shall see if he gets greedy, or if he is a man of his word.'

'How long have you known who I was?' Monty asked.

Bill laughed. 'Since you mysteriously arrived, but I was surprised the women helped you so easily. It made my job all the easier because I could watch you, without taking you in, which would have looked odd to the villagers, and awkward for business.'

'My business here is to catch one man. If that is not you then you have nothing to fear.'

'I'm no traitor,' he replied before Monty left him.

Bill waited until Monty had climbed out of the cellar before following. Monty made straight for the cottage; he had to retrieve the pistols and make his way to the headland. Lydia was in danger and he was just realising how much.

★　★　★

Emma had been selling pies for over an hour. She could not stop thinking about the way that Gregory had appeared within the village. He said he had men on the headland who could have got down quickly, but how? If he had arrived by boat they would have been seen by the smugglers, yet the man had managed to be in the heart of the village, so close to the inn and . . . the inn?

She looked to see if Annie were coming. That was it, the inn, there had to be a way into the village through there. She quickly saw to the remaining customers and then gathered up the coin and folded away the cloths. She must find Maisie if she could, but where to start? If the inn was central to their quest to find the traitor then Monty could be in grave danger. If Gregory was connected with Bill and Annie in some way then they knew he wasn't her Tommy. So what they thought of her made a shiver run down her spine. Then why were they letting, Monty work for them? It did not make sense to her. She looked around for inspiration and smiled as she saw the church behind her.

Going inside she saw a few people sitting in the pews quietly praying. She followed suit, then watched and waited for a sight of the clergy. Surely he would know the names of his flock, particularly a new and injured member. Some moments passed by before a lady started dusting and cleaning around the altar.

She approached gently, not wanting to appear brusque or anxious in any way.

'Excuse me,' she began.

'Yes, what is it?' the woman whispered, looking nervously up at a stained glass window with the apostle gazing down upon the congregation.

'I am trying to find a lady who is here with her sister. She has an injured leg and is called, Maisie. Do you know where I might find her?'

The woman looked around her and then smiled. 'You mean 'Maisie the daisy'?'

'Do I?'

'Yes, she's quite sweet really, but it ain't her leg that's crooked, it's her mind. She's in yonder asylum, love. Makes daisy chains and hums to herself all day long. She don't make any sense when she talks, so she hums. I know this, lass, because I clean in there too. Mind, don't you go telling folk as I gossiped about a patient.' The woman looked genuinely concerned.

'No, I won't and thank you.'

Emma left the church and returned to the stall to find an irate Annie standing with both fists firmly on her hips.

'I thought you'd run off with my takings, girl.'

'No, I just wanted to say a prayer for the coastguard and his family.' Emma tried to look sincere, whilst silently asking for understanding and forgiveness for lying to the woman. She passed the bag of coin to Annie.

'Well let's go and whet our throats before we return,' Annie said, and slapped an arm around Emma's shoulder.

'I'm not thirsty,' Emma told her, as it was obvious she was heading back to the inn.

'You're a bundle of fun to go anywhere with, do you know that?' Annie removed her arm. 'What do you want to do then?'

'Go for a walk by the river,' Annie replied, and smiled.

'Whatever takes your fancy, lass, but be back in an hour. I have to get the wagon back before my Bill needs it.'

'Yes, Annie, I will,' She ambled toward the river and waited for Annie to disappear inside the inn before she quickly made her way over the bridge and up to the heavy gates which led to the stark grey building that was the asylum.

14

Lydia looked at the pistol directed at her. She thought of fleeing but realised that would be folly.

'Enter, Madame,' the man ordered from his sick bed. The accent was unmistakable.

'Reverend Brampton, do you wish anything to eat or drink?' Lydia asked, sounding as calm as she could.

'Do not pretend, Madame. You have stumbled into my lair and broken my little 'charade'. I am no man of God, and you . . . must be the inquisitive Mrs Frinton.' He gestured with the gun that she enter the room and close the door behind her.

Reluctantly she did. He had one arm in a sling and was propped up in the Reverend's bed. It was obvious from the attire at the side of the bed that he had been there some time, and also that

Mrs Brampton was a regular visitor to him. A negligee had been thrown over a chair in the corner of the room.

Lydia had achieved her goal; she had made her way into the bedchamber, but now she asked herself, what should she do? More to the point, what could she do?

*　*　*

Emma waited anxiously as a servant answered the door. She was extremely nervous; these places were renowned for their cruelty and harshness. She expected to be greeted by a sickly aroma, and deafened by screams of pitiful souls restrained and defeated by a cruel system, but instead a lady with a neat white starched cotton cap, and pressed apron over a long grey dress, answered the door. Her highly polished hob nailed boots upon the stone-slab floor made more noise than any scream that emanated from within the walls.

Emma, aware that time and luck may be passing her by, did not hesitate in getting straight to the point. 'I have travelled all the way from Ebton to deliver a message to Mrs Maisie Ackton from a friend of hers. Would it be possible for me to see her forthwith?' She smiled as sweetly as she could, trying to appeal to the woman's good nature . . . hoping she had one.

'You may enter, but please remember this is a house of rest for troubled people. Please do not excite the lady should she wish to meet you.'

Emma nodded; the woman stepped back, allowing Emma to enter. 'What is your name?'

'Miss Emma Frinton,' she replied.

There were other similarly attired women. They had bunches of keys attached to their belts, but beyond this obvious sign of control there was no further symbol of restraint or people being displayed as in some of these institutions. Emma followed the woman along a whitewashed corridor and out through patio doors to the lawn at the rear of the building. Here a lady was bent over picking daisies.

'Stay here.' The lady approached the hunched figure slowly. 'Maisie, you have a young lady to see you. She has come all the way from Ebton to visit you.'

On hearing this, the woman's head shot up. She muttered something. The attendant shook her head. 'You make no sense, woman. I shall tell her to go away. She has wasted her time and . . . ' Maisie grabbed her skirt. 'Well, you behave then. She can stay a short time, but no grumbling and talking nonsense. You promise me that and I shall let her stay.'

Maisie nodded her agreement, and the attendant withdrew.

'You won't get any sense from her, but she is harmless enough.' She walked off.

Maisie was standing up straight. She had a half made daisy chain in her hand and stared straight at Emma who approached her slowly, and said in a quiet voice, 'I have come from Ebton, Maisie. I want to know what happened to you at the vicarage. Why are you here?' Emma's heart was pounding; she hoped she had not said too much but time ticked on.

'Why?' She stared at Emma, the chain slipped from her fingers and landed on the grass.

Emma bent down and picked it up. She looked at it fondly. 'It is very pretty.'

'Mmm, keep it,' Maisie said, and started picking more flowers.

'Why are you here? You are not mad, are you? Why did the Reverend's wife say that your leg was broken? Tell me, Maisie, because my mother is working in the vicarage, and I am frightened for her safety.' Emma crouched next to her and looked into the woman's watery eyes.

'Then she must leave there while she can. They killed him . . . ' Her voice trailed off and Emma at first thought she had heard wrongly.

'They killed who?' she asked, hoping not to panic the woman.

'I screamed and screamed and woke up here. I no longer know what I knew, you see. I saw, what I could not see. It was beyond my understanding. They killed him . . . my master, my friend . . . my . . . A good man, not like the harridan he married; her and her fancy man. They killed him . . . I saw, but couldn't help him. Nothing to be done. Too late. They locked me here. I screamed and screamed. I don't want to be out there. Don't let them send me away. I want to stay here. He's dead . . . in the cellar . . . my friend.' She sobbed.

'You and he were more than friends?' Emma asked, feeling pity for her, and trying to suppress the growing fear she felt inside her as she realised how much danger her mother was in.

Maisie nodded. 'Why not? His wife was a harlot, with her Frenchie fancy man. She made a fool of him. I loved him, he needed me, but I couldn't stop him going down there, and he saw them. Them and their friends,' she answered, shook her head and stared at a flower.

'What friends?' Emma placed a hand on Maisie's and the woman stroked it fondly.

'The villagers, the tunnel you see, only the Frenchie was interested in more than baccy and silk.'

Emma took in a deep breath. 'Maisie, I must go and warn my mother. Tell me, did you try to tell Mr Gregory Wild of the militia about what happened?'

Maisie chuckled. 'How, my sweet? Was I to walk fifteen miles whilst I screamed for my lost lover? Would he believe the ranting of a woman out of her head with grief?' She squeezed Emma's hand. 'No, lass, you go tell Mr Wild if you want to, but don't say I'd said it, or they'll put you next to me in here, so we may make mad rumblings and daisy chains together.'

'Maisie, I have to go now, but I will

return. I shall visit again and all will be well,' Emma promised.

'No, lass, nought will ever be well again. Visit if you wish, but leave Maisie here where they look after her and my days of graft are done.' She waved her good bye.

Emma responded, then made her way quickly to the door. She had to find Gregory, and quickly. Her mother was in a house with murderers, and Monty was also in danger if Mrs Brampton's friends were the villagers.

She ran over the bridge, her path blocked by Annie on the wagon.

'Whatever are you running from, Emma?'

'We have got to go to the barracks!' Emma said, as she climbed up onto the wagon's seat.

'Oh do we? And why would we be wanting to do such a mad thing as that, eh?' Annie glared at her; her cheeks were flushed from the ale house.

'Because I have discovered something that he must know. My mother is in danger and . . . '

Annie took the daisy chain from Emma's hand and ran it through her fingers. 'Now, what did I tell you, miss, about sticking your nose in business that don't concern you?'

Emma made to jump down from the wagon but Annie was strong and held onto her arm as she released the brake she led the wagon up the road and out of the town.

15

Monty wore the pistols and returned to the inn. This time he wasted no time on being humble, or engaging in any pretence.

'Bill, I need you in the cellar now.' He stepped behind the counter, not stopping to confront the man. Bending low to raise the hatch to the ladder, he was hindered when Bill's boot came firmly down upon it. Amos finished his tankard of porter and left the inn, sensing there was trouble brewing. Montgomery understood the way of them, no one wanted to bear witness to such, so they turned their heads away.

Monty glared at Bill. 'You either trust me on this and work together, or our friendship, tentative as it is, ends here. I am a man of position, Bill. I have enough knowledge about this village to wipe it and its inhabitants off the face of the map. If you do not wish to be a party to treachery then show me the way to the vicarage now!'

Bill looked at him as if considering his response. He leaned over and picked up a shillelagh. 'You were saying, 'Tommy'?'

'I was asking, are you with me or against me?' Monty did not flinch, he stared the man out.

'That's better, I don't like being threatened but I do like being asked. Here . . . ' He gave him the blackthorn club and lifted the hatch, then reached behind the small inn counter and retrieved something wrapped in an oil cloth. Once removed, it revealed a blunderbuss.

Monty raised an eye at the weapon. It was one that could do a great deal of harm and mutilation.

'It is amazingly persuasive.' He gestured for Monty to climb down. Once at the bottom he recovered the club and, with blunderbuss in one hand and club in the other, he walked over to the darkest corner of the cellar. There a fissure within the rock led to a cavern, from where a ladder had been made to a roughly hewn flight of steps within the rock.

'So from here you can hide the goods and then transport them at leisure from the vicarage, is that how it works?' Monty asked as he began to climb.

'Aye, that is how it used to, until the good Reverend took bad. Now we have your namesake crawling around here like he owns the headland, making demands and taking a cut of our hard earned lot.' The man had slung the gun across his back and climbed with no effort, such was his strength.

Bill pushed Monty flat against the rock and pointed the unloaded blunderbuss ahead of them. Silently they waited until the figure appeared.

⋆   ⋆   ⋆

Annie stopped the wagon once they were away from the town. Instantly,

Emma jumped down.

'So what yer going to do now, lass?' Annie looked at her as she stood defiantly facing her.

'I shall walk to the barracks if I have to because my mother is in danger and I will bring her help. And Monty, he . . . ' She stopped her words mid flow, realising that she had used his real name.

'Yes, you were saying? Monty, is it? So he your fancy man? Poor Tommy, whatever happened to him, eh? Found someone better already?' she laughed.

'I'm going to see Gregory Wild!' Emma replied and walked off down the road.

'You are a fool, Emma Frinton, a lovesick little fool,' Annie shouted after her.

Emma turned. 'No a valiant one!' she shouted back.

'Not from where I am standing. The barracks are over that way, about a mile away.'

Emma stopped.

'Come on, lass, tell me what Maisie has been telling you and we'll go see your Gregory, and heaven help you if I ends up in bother.' She waited for Emma to climb back up beside her.

Emma told her what had been said.

'Maisie don't speak sense. No one has had any sense out of her since she fell.' Annie shook her head. 'Why would she open up to you?'

'Because she trusted me, and my mother is in the house.' Emma saw a change of expression cross Annie's face.

'Hell's bells, if you is right, not even my Bill knows that the old b . . . priest is dead. He could be the next. What we wasting time chatting about. God help us!' Annie jolted the reins and, as fast as the vehicle would take them, they headed straight to the barracks.

★   ★   ★

Biddie screamed, her voice echoing around the cavern.

'Quiet, woman!' Bill snapped.

'You scared me half to death. Bill, she got into the room but she ain't come out and the missus is turning back on her walk. She could be a deadun already.' Biddie was breathless but still managed a flirtatious smile at Montgomery as she passed. 'My job's done now and I ain't going back.' She went on her way.

'You planted her there deliberately? You mean she wasn't there to wash linen?' Monty asked as he continued at speed to ascend the stairs.

'I had my suspicions but didn't want to get any village folk hurt.'

Monty looked back at him in disgust, lit by the lantern that Monty carried. The flickering light showed a nonchalant expression upon Bill's face. 'Thought I may as well let you strangers find out, seeing as how you'd come snooping in business that don't concern you.'

'Lydia could be hurt,' Monty said, and continued to climb.

'Yes, but then it was her idea to get involved, wasn't it?'

Monty said no more and soon found himself pushing up a trapdoor which led into the basement of the vicarage.

★ ★ ★

Gregory set off with his men, the wagon following behind. At last he had the French spy within his reach. The capture, the glory and the reward would go to him for once. This time, his brother could have the wench.

★ ★ ★

Lydia was told to sit on the window seat. She chatted in both French and English to the cad who rested in another man's bed, but that was the very least of his sins.

★ ★ ★

Mrs Brampton saw a woman's back resting against the window. She knew instantly who it was, and why she had been placed there. Her step quickened, the boat was ready, she and her lover would soon be gone from this land and a new chapter in her life would begin, where she would have a partner of her own age. She would love, live and be free of the constraints that had been inflicted upon her at an early age by her husband; a man two years younger than her own father. How she had grown to hate him and his sermonising.

★   ★   ★

Monty and Bill entered the house via the kitchens, silently making their way to the upper landing.

Monty looked at Bill and mouthed, 'Which door?'

Bill shrugged and responded in kind, 'How would I know?'

Monty glanced at the plaster work on the ceiling, and then at the number of doors — four either side of the central stairs. Whilst they were still trying to decide where to begin, the main door opened and shut with a bang. Both dropped to the shadows.

Mrs Brampton appeared on the stairs; she ran straight toward the door to the right of the stairs and knocked twice firmly before opening it.

'Henri!' she spoke as she entered the room.

Lydia glared at her. 'A traitor and a whore!'

'Save your words, woman. You can now help with the real task I need you for.' She took the gun off the Frenchman. 'Help him to his feet,' she smiled at the man, 'Jacques has arrived; he will be waiting on the tide in one hour.'

The injured man placed his weight upon Lydia using her as a crutch.

'We shall be away from here so soon, my love,' she spoke, as Lydia helped him to the top of the flight of stairs. Mrs Brampton followed with the pistol trained at Lydia's back.

Monty waited until they had reached the bottom step before coming out of the shadows. He had no wish for Lydia to fall on the stairs, especially whilst she supported such a burden. It was obvious the woman behind would not shoot her and risk injury to her lover as well.

'Hold!' he said, pointing both pistols at Mrs Brampton.

She was taken by surprise, turned and stumbled. The gun in her hand went off unexpectedly. Lydia and Henri fell to the ground, blood seeping onto the tiled floor beneath them.

Bill stood forward with the empty blunderbuss pointed at Mrs Brampton who let out an anguished scream and sank to her knees, crying for her Henri.

Monty reached Lydia who was trapped under the fallen spy.

'Is he dead?' she asked, as Monty helped her to her feet.

'Stunned, I think,' he replied.

There was a scream behind them, as Bill hauled Mrs Brampton to her feet. 'Shame, it would have saved the hangman a job, then.'

From outside the vicarage the scream was heard as Gregory dismounted. He and three militiamen burst into the house, pistols at the ready, to be faced by a fait accompli.

'Damnation, man, could you not have waited?' He slapped Monty on the back, resigned to the fact that his brother had once again become the hero of the hour.

'Where is Emma?' the joint question from Monty and Lydia made the man laugh.

'She will be here any moment with the old Nag from the inn.' He did not say any more but smiled as the two stepped back from the fallen man.

'See to this, Gregory, there's a good chap. I want to return to our home for one last night of rest before we go back to London and my home.'

'The one in Mayfair or Kent, Monty?' Gregory asked with mock bitterness.

Monty looked down at Lydia's surprised face. 'Mayfair first, I have to present my report to Horse Guards. We have to make him fit to travel; he is to go back to France, in exchange for a very important man.'

Lydia gave him a squeeze, her eyes watering, as they heard the wagon pull up outside. Lydia ran through the doorway to meet her daughter.

'What about her?' Bill glanced at the pathetic creature who sobbed at his feet.

'She is a murderer and a traitor, what do you think,' Gregory said.

Monty stepped outside.

★   ★   ★

Emma saw Monty and rushed to him, wrapping her arms around him. 'It's all right, Emma. Your father will be freed. We can go back to the cottage tonight. There will be transport sent for us tomorrow.' He hugged her close.

She looked up into his dirt smudged

face. 'What of us, Montgomery Wild? What shall we do?'

'Oh, I think an introduction to my mother is imminent. Mind, after this little adventure it may seem slightly less of a challenge than it otherwise would have been.' He smiled at one and then the other of the two women. 'You shall both be pampered and cosseted and, after we have your father home, we shall show you the town and, if he is willing, an announcement will be made of our engagement, Miss Frinton.' He looked at Lydia. 'If that meets with your approval.'

'Emma?' she asked.

'Absolutely,' she answered, although no reply was needed.

'Then let us go home,' Lydia said, and they began to walk back down the headland path to the small town in which so much of their lives had changed.